Journey to Jamestown

ELIAS'S STORY

KINGFISHER
a Houghton Mifflin Company imprint
222 Berkeley Street
Boston, Massachusetts 02116
www.houghtonmifflinbooks.com

First published in 2005
2 4 6 8 10 9 7 5 3 1

LIBRARY OF CONGRESS CATALOGING-IN-PUBLICATION DATA
has been applied for.

ISBN 0-7534-5796-2
ISBN 978-07534-5796-2

Printed in India
1TR/0105/THOM/SGCH/90NS

MY SIDE OF THE STORY

Journey to Jamestown

ELIAS'S STORY

LOIS RUBY

KINGFISHER
BOSTON

Read Elias's story first, then flip over
and read Sacahocan's side of the story!

Chapter One

Jamestown Colony, Virginia. January, 1608.

"Cut, lad!" said Master Whitman.

I felt the man's skin yield to my knife. I shouldn't have looked into his pleading eyes.

Master Whitman grabbed the lancet, nicking my thumb. He made a neat slit in the belly of Thomas Barker. Beads of blood turned to a thin stream. I swooned, sure I'd fall like a log.

"Ye'll *never* be a surgeon, boy, if ye can't make a simple cut to flow the malevolent fluids of this sufferer. Can ye at least fetch the bowl?"

Thomas's eyes were pinched shut as Master Whitman squeezed the wound to release a greenish trickle into the bowl.

"Ach, why'd I ever take ye on?" Master Whitman muttered.

Myself, I wondered why I'd tied my fate to this barber-surgeon without a kind bone under his skin. I was more suited to the work of a shopkeeper or a grave digger, for I could no more cut into a man's flesh than grow chives on my chin.

Yet what choice had Mother left me, widowed and scratching by, with three daughters ripe for marriage—and not one pretty enough to catch a lad's eye. We were as poor as beggars. So I, Elias Ridpath, barely 13, found myself apprenticed to Edward Whitman.

Mother had hurried me to the dock, soaking her cuffs with tears. "This is your chance, Eli. Barber-surgeons don't starve, eh? There's no glory in starvation." More tears. "Lucky for us Master Whitman is desperate for an apprentice before he sails to Virginia. Lucky," she repeated, shoving into my arms a stale bundle of bread, two shriveled apples, and a few sweetmeats.

Master Whitman had been waiting for us, tapping his timepiece with long, crooked fingers. "First lesson, promptness. You're two minutes late."

Mother dipped her head. "Sorry, sir, it is my fault entirely." She ran her fingers through my mop of copper curls, gently inching me toward the doctor. "Elias is a bright boy, sir. Soaks up whatever you teach him like thirsty muslin. And prompt. Aren't you, son? Prompt as the tides." She backed away. My heart sank like a stone. Would I ever see her again or taste her ginger cakes warm from the oven?

Sailing across the Atlantic, Master Whitman pummeled me with facts about our barbering and doctoring business and with advice about the new world we were gliding toward.

"Beware the Virginia savages, boy. Look at them

cross-eyed, and they'll tie you to a tree. They'll peel the skin off your back and toss it into their infernal fires until it sizzles like bacon. Mark my words."

That was *not* promising news during the endless gray days at sea. We had little work during the crossing. Mostly we shaved men who'd been afflicted with creepy-crawly lice, which was enough to turn my stomach, already knotted with loneliness. I longed for home each night, folded into my hammock that swung amid a dozen men. I'd sooner have slept among the livestock in the hold, sniffing cattle, rather than overripe humans belching beer and reeking for want of a wash.

But, as Mother said, we were lucky. There were some 60 passengers aboard, none requiring surgery. Some were green with seasickness—I the greenest of all, my head hung over the rail, begging for a quick burial at sea. Some of the men had fevers, which Master Whitman treated with mysterious potions that smelled fierce. The boots I peeled off each night smelled sweeter.

At last, after four months of waves lapping the deck, one of the eagle-eyed crew members spotted land. Heart thrumming, I squinted my eyes to spot the savages that would dot the shoreline. I imagined the captain sending Mother the sausage casing that had once been me with a note pinned to it: *Welcome home the hide of Elias Ridpath, who survived the wretched voyage only to be skinned alive by wanton savages.*

We trudged ashore on wobbly sea legs, with Master Whitman shoving me ahead of him. No Indians. In the fading dusk, I saw only the shadows of primitive huts and lean settlers who were none too eager to welcome us. I nearly hung on Master Whitman's coattails. The settlers must have thought me an ugly growth on his backside.

We settled into our tent without so much as a scrap of bread.

"You'll be the scourge of me," Master Whitman muttered as he nailed canvas sheeting between his cot and my bed of hardened dirt. Never had I spent a more desolate night. Already I missed the foul men in the ship's hammocks and longed for home, so far away.

Night dragged by until . . .

"Wake, boy!" Master Whitman jabbed me with the blunt end of a lancet. "We have business to conduct." He lit a fat candle that fluttered across the miserable face of poor Thomas Barker, and thus our surgery business began.

After the cutting Master Whitman placed a poultice on the wound and left the patient to steal relief in sleep. It didn't happen. The man's tossing troubled me all night as I lay awake beside his cot. Even a thin mat between the dirt floor and me might have helped—but no such luxury. Master Whitman, of course, slept like a lamb on the other side of the curtain.

Finally, as the sky was brightening, Thomas Barker mercifully fell silent, and I slept.

He was out of his misery when the sun rose on that crisp autumn morning. We carried him out to a ravine where already a half-dozen men awaited burial. Was there a lad who'd be checking each returning ship for sight of Thomas Barker, as I used to do for my father? Hours before my seafaring pa drew his last breath he'd whispered, "You're a fine, tender scout, son, but you're a fish on a hook wiggling this way and that."

Sick at heart, I resolved that this strange land would not defeat me. Not Elias Ridpath, not myself! Time to wriggle no longer. So, on the morning of January 3, 1608 I resolved to become the best barber-surgeon the new world would ever see—if the *malevolent fluids* that energized Master Whitman didn't unsettle me and send me toppling like a wood-rotted gate.

Chapter Two

Hammering woke me on my second morning in Jamestown. I found myself under a brilliant sky amid a hodgepodge of buildings surrounded by trees. Their reddish leaves fluttered to the ground at my feet. A horse trotted across the clearing, tethered by a boy a notch shorter than myself.

"I'm not born for this rubbish!" shouted a man hanging from a makeshift ladder.

"But George," said the boy, "you heard Captain Smith: 'He that will not work shall not eat.'"

"What's there to eat? We're all starving like London curs."

A hammer flew out of the man's hand, and I gave it back to him.

He turned full around. "Who's this?"

"Elias Ridpath, sir, apprentice to Master Whitman."

"The leech? We heard about him before he graced our shores. God save you."

I doffed my cap.

"A gentleman is he, Bones, hat and all?"

Embarrassed, I tucked the cap under my arm. "I'm comforted to see that there are other lads here." Bones—curious name.

"You and me's the only ones without whiskers.

No girls," he said forlornly.

I'd had enough of sisters back home. Breakfast held more interest. "Sir, where can I get a shank of bread?"

George laughed. "If there's a place, lad, tell us. We're reduced to eating roots and who knows whot that's growing around here. Haven't chewed meat since June."

"Welcome to the Starving Time," said Bones.

I swallowed a wad of spit. Breakfast?

Chestnut ropes hung to Bones's collar, more hair than such a rodentlike face deserved. The horse's mane looked puny by comparison. I imagined the snick-snick of Master Whitman's clippers attacking that mess. "What are you building, sir?"

George sat at the top of the ladder. "Tinderbox houses. Tell him, Bones."

"One blast of winter wind—"

"Look at these sticks that the captain calls a house."

I stood dead center in a triangular colony of some 40 structures. Half-built clapboard houses with thatched roofs circled the perimeter, and a few tents leaned into the wind.

"'Keep building,' they say. Tell him, Bones."

"More's coming."

"Like he says, sixty came with you, and more's on their way to this God-forsaken plot of earth. Yessir, if the wind sends a spark over here, the whole colony's gone in a lick of flames."

"Food supplies, too." Bones patted his belly, caved in like a spoon.

And me complaining of hunger after just one day.

"Charred flesh falling off the bones," George said, with more glee than such a dire prediction merited.

How to doctor burns? Mother smeared us with lard, but we still blistered something fierce. Mother! A pang of longing stabbed my chest. The horse looked on; he didn't care.

George motioned to a palisade of thick, upright logs three times my height. "Tell him what's the wall for, Bones."

"Savages."

"Indians wild as tigers. The wall's so's we can sight 'em coming and be ready with our muskets and falconets."

"Good eye for a shot, our George," Bones boasted.

"Else end up an Indian's pincushion."

"Sir?"

Master Whitman splashed brackish water on his face and scraped a razor across his rutted cheek as he growled, "You've brought me to this no-man's-land."

What? It was he who brought me to this inhospitable land without food! I knew I'd best be careful, for my master twisted the truth to suit him. "Sir, if someone was to suffer burns, what would we do for it?"

"Slather on a paste of tallow and honey, if we've got a gob. Ashes, otherwise. Cover it with skin."

"Skin, sir?"

"Lizard skin, but I doubt there are lizards here. Bound to be frogs in these marshes."

Rancid lard sounded sweeter. Doubts about being a good barber-surgeon jabbed me, especially with my belly squawking for a nibble. At home, poor as we were, there was always a heel of bread or a potato. Now I peeked out of our tent and saw men sluggishly swinging hammers or leaning against the new buildings, skin and bones themselves.

Curious. Weren't the forests teeming with all manner of plants and birds and squirrels? Wouldn't there be fish swarming in the river? Sturgeon big as rowboats? Why was everybody starving?

I ventured out to explore.

"You're Whitman's boy." A voice boomed from thin lips surrounded by a mustache and a beard as red as mine would be one day.

George nodded toward the man, keeping the hammer clanging against the anvil. "Morning, Captain Smith." A chorus of other laborers joined him.

Captain Smith looked better fed than the others,

stocky and none too tall. His fierce blue eyes darted everywhere. Gave my stomach a turn, they did. Yet he looked just the way I'd look 15 years down the road. He saw it too.

"You, Rusty-Top, are we kin? What's your name?"

"Elias Ridpath, sir."

"No Ridpaths in the family." He turned to a man lolling under a tree. "Dobbin, have you no work?"

Mr. Dobbin hoisted himself to his haunches and thrust a red thumb under the captain's nose. "Can't labor, so afflicted, Captain. Something stung me. See? It's festered."

The captain called me over. "Whitman's boy, what can you do for him?"

Absolutely nothing, Captain. I don't know a swollen thumb from a kettle of rum. Terrified, I took hold of Mr. Dobbin's hand and examined it fore and aft. The hot thumb throbbed in my hand. I led him into the tent where Master Whitman sprawled on his cot, cleaning his nails with a penknife.

"This is Captain Smith, sir."

Whitman sprang to his feet. "Welcome to my humble dispensary, Captain."

"And Mr. Dobbin. His thumb's as hot and thick as a sausage."

"Time ye learned something, boy." Whitman

swiped the knife across his shirt. "Won't take a minute, Captain." He locked Mr. Dobbin's arm under his own and squeezed it as if he was wringing out the wash, until that thumb was raw-meat red and beating like a heart. Whitman dragged the poor victim to the door for better light. "Ah, a filament embedded in here." He sliced the thumb open.

"Aieee!" Mr. Dobbin bellowed. "Lord above!"

Whitman sucked on the wound, spitting blood and whatnot onto the floor.

Bile rose in my throat and went no farther. One advantage of an empty stomach.

"There, good as new." Whitman smeared ointment on the thumb and dropped the arm like a dead raccoon. "Here, boy, wrap him."

I bound Mr. Dobbin's thumb and whispered, "Keep it clean." That's what Mother always warned. The captain looked on with a stronger stomach than my own.

Mr. Dobbin staggered away. Would he be dead in the morning, like my first patient?

He wasn't, but he was not yet eager to swing an ax or muck out the stables. Captain Smith had no patience for sloth. He trod around yelling orders. Satisfied that all were toiling like beasts of burden, he brought a bowl of onion soup to our tent.

"Payment for services rendered," he said. When Master Whitman drew the bowl to his mouth, Captain Smith yanked it away. "The boy needs it worse." I slurped that tasty soup, watching my master's hungry eyes over the rim of the bowl. The pulpy onions felt mighty good sliding down my throat, and my belly welcomed them like old friends.

I didn't know how hollow my innards would be in another month and how my skin would sag for want of flesh beneath it.

Chapter Three

George and Bones were my only friends. The others saw me as a stray cat, grubbing for scant bits of food.

Though Bones was as thin as a goose, his unflagging cheerfulness amazed me, especially after George gave me remnants of Bones's life before Jamestown. A mother he barely remembered abandoned him in a charnel house, where a barmaid spotted him lurking around at a funeral. It was she who dubbed him Bones since he was all skinny angles and little flesh. She took him home to her parents, and he happily starved with them for years. But when she married a penniless ragman, her family tossed him out again in a torrential storm. Drenched to his namesake bones, he wandered to the docks where he collided with a man puffing his last smoke on firm land before sailing for the New World. That was George.

The Jamestown men jabbered endlessly about women. Around the night fire they danced a jig, stretching a kerchief between two men. One would twirl and step lightly, pretending to swish a skirt. Raucous laughter followed, with the men swigging what ale was left in our kegs and then stumbling off to bed. Jamestown needed the gentleness of women like my mother and sisters. Master Whitman was my only family here—and him without a comforting word on his tongue as we clipped away at the shaggy men lined up outside our tent. Enough hair landed at our feet to stuff a mattress. My haircuts left each man looking like his ears had been sewn on at different heights. Truth is, I was more interested in the surroundings of the camp than those dirty heads—especially the men patrolling the top of our palisade.

One morning there was an unusual rustling at the wall.

"What's happening?" I asked my haircut victim, Master Rysdale.

"Sighted some savages, no doubt, smelling blood."

"Excuse me, sir." I left Rysdale half done and scrambled to the top of the church to see what I could. Three Indians neared our fort!

"Move a muscle, red man, and I'll blow yer brains out." This from Master Collins, aiming a gun point-blank at one of the Indians. Good! We were well protected from these marauding savages. But now one took a step forward, and gunfire blasted the calm morning air. I saw the bloody hole widening in the Indian's chest before he collapsed.

Never had I seen a man bleed to death before. My own blood pumped wildly in my ears at the horror of it.

The other two natives retreated, but then I saw another Indian, a girl, slip down a tree, and God forgive, I prayed she'd get away before Master Collins's bullets found her.

Badly shaken, I slid down from the roof and returned to Master Rysdale.

"Called to the privy, were you?" he grumbled.

I murmured a quick *yessir* and tried to even up his hair with trembling hands.

"Whot's this?" said George, next for a haircut. "Whot's a savage doing in civilized country?"

I spun around to see a boy in the clearing and ventured closer, thinking of the Indian with the hole in his chest. How had this one gotten past the guards? He looked harmless enough, some five years old, naked as the day he was hatched and brown as a Christmas goose.

Mr. Dobbin crept up to grab him. I shouted, "Let him be!" The child's eyes flamed wide, and he ran into my arms. Bones draped his own shirt around the lad.

"Are you lost?" I asked. No answer.

"Them savages don't speak the king's tongue," said Mr. Rysdale.

I didn't know the tongue he was speaking, save that he kept repeating one word that sounded like "monkey."

Captain Smith jostled his way through the crowd. "Pamunkee, lad? One of Chief Opechancanough's urchins?" Something flickered in the boy's eyes.

What a disturbance that raised. Everybody spouted an opinion:

"Reckon we ought to be getting him back? It's the Christian thing to do."

"And get ourselves scalped? You daft?"

Captain Smith said, "The Pamunkee will attack as soon as they know we've got the boy."

"Those barbarians'll think we kidnapped the waif."

"They don't reason like civilized folk. They shoot first, ask questions after."

"Poisoned arrows, you can bet, aimed for the heart of an Englishman."

"I say we use him as a shield against those marauders."

"Hear! Hear!"

"Even savages wouldn't kill their own, aye?"

"Don't count on it," Captain Smith groused.

The Indian boy shuddered in my arms. "Captain, sir, he's scared. He needs to get back to his people."

"Did I ask you, lad?"

I whispered to the boy, poking my chest, "I'm Elias. You?" I patted his chest until his face lit up.

"Quangatarask." He repeated it until I said it right.

I tapped Captain Smith's shoulder, level with my own. "His name's Quangatarask, sir."

Captain Smith said with a wry smile, "Ready for battle, little man?" That only drove him farther into the hollow of my belly.

Then, out of the clearing, appeared the Indian girl I'd seen in the tree. She wore a loose cloth tied over one shoulder. The other shoulder was bare, showing colorful markings. Golden limbs hung out of the sleeves and hem of her dress. Her feet were shoeless and crusted with dirt. My sisters would be mortified to appear in public that way!

"Beware," George whispered. "They send a scout, and warriors'll swarm over us in no time."

The brazen girl marched into our camp and snatched Quangatarask out of my arms. "My brother."

He spun around to her.

Captain Smith said, "You speak English, do you?"

She nodded over Quangatarask's head.

"Splendid. Take your brother home and explain to the kindly Chief Opechancanough that we didn't steal him, he merely wandered into our camp. Is that clear?"

She nodded again, watching me with puzzling eyes the blue-gray color of the ocean, not black raisins like her brother's eyes. Also, her hair was much lighter than his. Something about the shape of her nose and the surprise of a few freckles across her cheeks reminded me of my sister Catherine. But how could a savage girl look *anything* like my sisters?

The next day she was back, flanked by Quangatarask. I'd been helping Bones whitewash the Anglican church when the two Indians came up behind us, silent as snow. My heart flip-flopped as I remembered the dire warnings.

Quangatarask tugged on my shirt. "Ly-iss, Ly-iss."

I jumped off the scaffold, backing away warily.

"I come to thank you." The lass's voice was soft, her English clipped.

"How is it you know my language when I can't mumble a word in yours?"

She shook her head, clearly unwilling to answer my question, and I knew I wasn't to ask it again. But still, I wondered.

"My people have visited your camp," she said. "They tell me you are the healer."

"Hardly so. I can't even stand the sight of blood."

"My people say you came with the medicine man."

"Aye. Master Whitman." How did she know about me? Indian spies? *Don't trust them.*

Something fluttered from her hands. I whipped my own away. She sighed. "Only tobacco leaves. Boil. Drink the juices to ease pains." She pointed to her head, her teeth, her knees, as the English words wouldn't come to her. She handed me a tangle of roots. "Snakeroot. Chew for fever." Turning to leave, she pivoted Quangatarask on her hip.

"What's your name?"

"Sacahocan. I am a healer among my people, like you."

"I know nothing, and my teacher isn't very good."

Sacahocan smiled. "You are born with the spirit to heal. You see with a third eye."

I clapped my hand to my forehead. "No eye there."

"The eye is inside your head. You will see."

"Wait! Can I talk to Quangatarask?"

"No."

The word, sharp as a hound's tooth, made my jug-shaped ears hot.

"My brother speaks few words. He does not learn like other boys."

I called his name. Quangatarask put both palms out as we schoolmates had done when the teacher wielded a hickory stick. I had no thought to strike him. I put my palms over his and then flipped my hands over. We went top to bottom until Sacahocan said,

"Come. The sun is low in the sky." She handed me the basket that had been at her feet. It was heavier than I expected, throwing me off balance.

"Corn. Your people are hungry."

I wanted to protest—*taking food from natives?*—but she was gone as silently as she'd come.

What a feast we had that night, sinking our teeth into corn roasted crisp over the fire, but there weren't enough ears to go around, and those on the outer circle cursed us. Never had I felt so guilty and so deserving at the same time.

"Just a matter of time before the savages come," Captain Smith said, passing up a beautiful, crisp ear of corn.

Chapter Four

What abomination have ye brought into my dispensary?" Master Whitman stormed out of our tent, waving the tangle of snakeroot, which he tossed into the circle cleared for the dice game we played when Reverend Mr. Storch wasn't around.

I jumped to my feet, dice hidden in my palm.

"Roll, lad," said George, but nothing short of a bee sting could have pried my hand open.

"Snakeroot, from the Indian girl, sir. For ague, when a man's burning up with fever."

"For ague?" he bellowed. "There's but one thing for ague, and etch this into your pea-soup brain. A man goes alone to a crossroad. As the clock begins to strike midnight, he turns around thrice and pounds a nail into the ground. Before the twelfth is struck, he walks backward from the nail, and the ague is gone."

George laughed. "You don't say, Master Whitman. And where's it go?"

Master Whitman threw a glare that would shrivel a carrot. "Into the nail until the next man steps on it, and then he's the poor drunkard rattling with fever. A known fact."

Which he just made up.

George snorted. "Fact, aye? Roll, lad," he said, coaxing the dice out of my hand.

Each morning another man or two staggered toward our tent and collapsed at my feet as if Master Whitman had a magical cure for starvation like his hocus-pocus for ague. Sad to see, more men lay stacked in burial mounds around the palisade than slept in beds.

Captain Smith called us, his untidy militia, out onto the parade ground. The men stewed under the midday sun with wool underbreeches chafing their skin beneath all that metal. I thought of Sacahocan with her limbs bared to the autumn breeze and the boy, my word, naked as a cannonball.

"Men of Jamestown, you're a motley lot," the captain shouted.

"Aye," said Master Rysdale, "but we staved off the bloodthirsty savages come to avenge their scout's unfortunate death."

"How many of our own did we lose in that muddled struggle?" the captain demanded of us.

"Two, sir!" answered Bones eagerly.

Captain Smith glared at him. "Men, stand straight for king and country!" Came the clatter of mail and armor and scabbards as men weak from famine struggled to stand tall. "You know nothing of farming and less of hunting. As for fish, unless they leap from the river into your pot, you go hungry. Gentlemen, bah. Give me warriors any day or at least a man who can charm a few greens out of this sandy soil." He poked the toe of his boot into the ground. "You can't even grow worms."

The sun beat down. Being fair skinned, I wished I'd worn a cap to keep my head from crisping like goose fat. Cheek to jowl—and downwind besides—the stench was ripe and heady. What I wouldn't have given for a naked dip in the river, like the natives. But our water swarmed with bugs and frogs and was barely drinkable without infested men shedding skin in its shallows.

Captain Smith ranted on, ". . . no choice but to trade with our savage neighbors."

The men groaned, rattling their swords.

"They're clever farmers and hunters with no end to their food supplies, as young Elias will attest, having managed to get us a bushel of corn. So, who will queue up behind me?" No one moved. "George Tyding? You've a keen eye for a target." He snapped his fingers, and George ambled over. "Very well, gentlemen, I shall volunteer you." Every fifth man became a trader, myself included, to which Whitman muttered, "Good riddance."

"Boy, you have this night to learn how to treat

arrow wounds," Captain Smith barked. By sunrise, I'd be on a barge with seven others headed for the village of Werowocomoco, deep in Powhatan territory. My knobby knees buckled at the captain's latest bulletin: "Mind, the great Chief Powhatan's none too hospitable to English guests."

Master Whitman grudgingly gave me a medicine bag for the trip, with hurried instructions. Waving a pair of pliers, he explained, "If a man be shot with an arrow or, God spare, a gun, use these to pull out the offending projectile while a compatriot boils oil."

"What kind of oil, sir?"

"Bear fat's best or deer and boiled to bubbling to pour over the wound."

Ouch! I drew in my breath.

"The patient will caterwaul like a witch, but the blistering heals the wound. Unless, of course, the poor wretch succumbs."

Dies. I let out the breath, light-headed.

"Don't be maudlin, boy. Here." He gave me bandages to wet and apply to stab wounds, apothecary jars with scribbled instructions for treating the bloody flux or dropsy swellings, a bevy of glass cups for suctioning muscular poisons, and a blood-encrusted knife. "For God's sake, don't be reluctant if a man's in need of the lancet." He stuffed a diagram of the human body into my bag. "So's you'll know where everything is inside before you cut—and no jagged cuts, mind. Straight as an apple slice."

Thus did I, blood-squeamish coward, become a field surgeon. Mercy on my patients!

We camped on the rocky ground along the James river. The first morning, the sun barely poking its head over the horizon, a rustling in the trees woke me. One of our own, relieving himself? A count of the sleeping mounds around me tallied all seven. I dug the crust out of my eyes, prepared to yell *bear!* and run for the water. Weren't bears poor swimmers?

Instead I spotted a boy near my age with a tangle of yellow hair whipping across his face.

"Hallo!" I called, but he streaked away.

George said, "Waking the devil's own, are you?"

"A boy, in the trees!" I whispered breathlessly.

"Indian scout. They've eyes everywhere."

"This was an English boy, fair and blond as my sister Mary."

"Dressed like us?"

"No, barefoot, just a breech at the waist, flapping in the breeze."

George sat up. "Then it's true whot they say. There's some of 'em left."

"Who, sir?"

"There was English here before us, but they vanished like smoke, they did, without a trace."

"They left a trace. That boy. Let's find him."

"He doesn't want to be found, Elias. Else, why'd he scamper away like a scared doe?"

We marched ashore near the village of Werowococomo, muskets drawn, and me with a paltry medicine bag lapping against my chest as my only weapon. We were a party of eight: Captain Smith, six timorous soldiers rattling armor and armaments, and one callow medic, whose knees knocked like shaken dice. We might as well have blown a bugle announcing our arrival for all the surprise we presented.

Indians surrounded us, bows drawn!

Chapter Five

My blood beat in my ears as if I'd already been shot. I pictured an arrow through my chest . . . I'd fall on it, and it'd stick out my back. No way to yank it out without pulling my heart along with it. I clutched my chest and shifted my eyes to the captain without moving my head. It would also have an arrow through it, ear to ear. Which would kill me first?

"Don't let them smell your fear," Captain Smith said.

I reeked. Taking a deep breath—probably my last—I studied the enemy. Feathers and shells swung from holes in their ears. Animal-skin cloths barely covered the necessary. Their bare chests glistened, as though rubbed with fat, sporting markings of snakes and horned deer amid painted swirls in red and black, as did their fearsome faces. These would be the last faces I'd see, haunting me through eternity.

Some among us murmured prayers, but Captain Smith stood calm. We dead were prodded into the village in a circle of Indians. Only the jagged rock that tore into my boot convinced me that I was still alive.

"Party's not over yet," George whispered.

Captain Smith's mouth smiled—but his eyes did not—as he said through clenched teeth, "Silence, if you value your scalps."

They led us into a long house made of sticks and bark, with skins for door flaps. I coughed in the smoke that billowed from a fire in the center and stung my eyes. Gasping for air, I followed the smoke trailing upward to a hole in the roof. Drummers pounded relentlessly. Painted men, heads covered with bird feathers, danced around the fire, tossing dried leaves into it.

We marched to a throne where sat Wahunsenacah, Chief Powhatan. Easy to see why they called him the great chief, as power rolled off him in waves. He rose, huge as a bear and covered in a bulky raccoon-skin cloak with the tails hanging to his ankles. Captain Smith stood eye level with the chief's beating heart. A thick rope of gray hair stretched across his head and hung like a horse's tail over his left shoulder. Wisps of gray dotted his chin—hardly a beard by English standards—but what he lacked in whiskers he replaced with pearls, painted shells, and copper baubles hanging around his neck, heavy enough to drag a lesser man's head down.

The cold eyes of his greyhound inspected us as he paraded on sinewy legs, his hind end proud and lean. He sniffed at Captain Smith, who offered a morsel of something from his pocket. A warrior snatched the morsel from the Captain's hand and tossed it into the fire. Did he think we meant to poison the chief's hound? A low, angry growl rumbled from the dog's belly. I'd growl too if I'd come that close to a treat and had it whipped away.

George huddled near me. The chief's eyes searched us, every man, and then a mirthless smile crossed his face.

"Again we meet, Captain Smith?"

The captain responded in the Powhatan language. They mangled each other's languages, while some 100 men sat on benches along the north wall and an equal number of women along the south wall, all of them chanting in a dizzying rhythm.

Chief Powhatan announced, "I speak your tongue better than you speak mine. We talk in white man's language."

"Worthy friend," Smith began, "we've brought you beads the color of the sky." Bentley stepped forward and rained blue beads before Chief Powhatan.

The chief touched them with his toes. "And?"

Bentley drew forth several rippling sheets of copper. Captain Smith said, "We know you prize this beautiful metal to form trinkets for your warriors so they may be favored with victory in battle."

Against us! Our men shifted from foot to foot, rattling armor. Suddenly I knew the sorry truth. While our weapons were mightier, the Indians would best us in battle because our soldiers were inexperienced and weighted down with breastplates, helmets, and shields, while theirs were nimble, trained as warriors and silent besides. Not at the moment, though. The drum beating quickened, and the chanting grew frenzied, along with the hissing and clacking of gourd rattles.

"And?" Chief Powhatan said again.

Bentley handed the chief three gleaming hatchets.

"We would not insult you with treasures beneath your dignity," Smith said, oily as a fish's innards.

"What do you want?" the chief asked.

"One hundred bushels of corn and wheat, a dozen turkeys and ducks, squash, potatoes, deer meat, little else," Captain Smith said casually, as though our skin and bones weren't hanging on these victuals.

The chief kicked at the heel of one of our muskets. "You bring fire sticks?"

"Worthy friend, I cannot spare what few we have, embattled as we are by the Spanish, who are approaching our shores at this very minute."

"Worthy friend," the chief mimicked, "I cannot spare what little we have, embattled as we are by the English, who are stealing our land at this very minute."

"Understood, good sir. I leave you with this wampum," Captain Smith said, "and I shall dispatch to you twenty fire sticks when our shipment arrives within the next moon, sir."

Powhatan weighed this promise. Was he a man of honor, like our captain, and trusting besides?

A grin spread across his leathery face. He signaled for the women at the west door to bring baskets brimming with the dried blackberries and plums and crocks of steaming hominy, oysters, and clams. Others ladled a fragrant wild turkey stew out of the pots slung over the fire.

"Feast with us while my men load your barge with good and plenty," Chief Powhatan said, and we dug in heartily. That night I enjoyed my first bellyache in nearly a month.

We slept fitfully in the enemy camp. Our beds were thick mats, with smooth deerskin comforters on our backs. George sprawled beside me, his head on a stone pillow and all but his nose and eyes covered.

I whispered, "You see? They're not savages after all."

"Just wait," George replied, reaching out to his musket beside him.

Chapter Six

The next morning in the Werowocomoco tent Mr. Bentley woke with a face as swollen as a rotten melon. "It's my tooth beating like a drum."

I panicked. "What do I do for it?"

"You're Whitman's apprentice," Bentley mumbled.

"The throbbin' tooth's got to come out, lad," George said, handing me the medical bag.

Trembling, I loosened the ties and dug around for—what? The lancet, the pliers, and *then* what?

Blood. There'd be buckets of it if the tooth wrenched free.

George held Mr. Bentley's mouth open, showing gums puffy and brown. *Now or never.* I straddled Mr. Bentley and reached in with the pliers, willing my elbow to hold still, my shaking fingers to clamp those pliers firmly over the tooth. Why had I ever left London's merry streets?

I had no luck. George handed me the lancet with an encouraging nod, and so, heaving a sour breath, I cut the gums around Bentley's tooth. His eyes swam, feet kicked, arms flailed, gutteral screams rose from his throat. George turned his eyes away but held Bentley's head firmly in the vise of his two arms. The tooth gleamed white in the red pool flooding

Bentley's mouth. I handed George the lancet; he slapped the pliers into my hand in exchange. Pressing my knee into Bentley's chest, I swallowed waves of fear and twisted and yanked until I'd won the prize.

Bently yelped like a mad cur and would have slugged me if George hadn't grabbed the poor wretch's arm.

To staunch the gushing blood, I tore a piece of cloth off the bottom of my own shirt, rolled it tight, and packed the gaping hole in Bentley's mouth. "Bite down hard," I commanded, sounding sure, though I wasn't.

Cold. Once I'd plunged a festering toe into a near-frozen river. The pain had vanished. On a bench near us sat a water pitcher crusted with overnight ice. I tore another strip off my shirt and scooped ice crystals, rolled and tucked the freezing wad against Mr. Bentley's cheek, and tied a makeshift bandage around his face. His grateful eyes thanked me, and I was overwhelmed with pride.

Done, I sank back on my heels, Bentley's blood sticky and drying on my hands. I chanced to see the pliers still locked around their catch. I swear, that tooth was as long as a finger and uglier than wood rot.

Throughout the miserable days on the river during our

return we breathed its icy fumes and stumbled over one another in the shallop. We went ashore to catch a few hours of sleep, ever alert for savages and wild animals. Such beasts didn't roam the streets of London. Robbers and half-crazed beggars, yes, but not horned bucks or coiled snakes. A thousand times I wished I was as brave and confident as Captain Smith. Nothing scared the man, though I doubt he'd have been able to pull Mr. Bentley's tooth.

Bentley looked like a squirrel hiding nuts in his cheek for a day or two, but he healed and slapped my back to thank me for relieving his agony. Was it possible I might be a healer, as that Indian girl had said?

Back in Jamestown, we found more dead and a fevered pox raging among the 60 souls left. The sick house was stacked threefold with cots, reeking of decay.

Master Whitman grumbled, "I've tended the sick day and night, and ye've been off sporting. Why, I ought to send ye back to England with the next transport."

I wished he would! But I just rolled up my sleeves and began washing the feverish men and spooning water between their parched lips. Dirty water.

Over their moaning, though Whitman was none too open to chatting, I ventured, "Sir, is it good for these men to swallow filthy river water?"

"If you're thirsty enough, you'll drink even your own fluids," he muttered.

My stomach lurched. Never! "But sir, I was thinking we should boil the water. Let the sediment sink to the bottom and give the men what rose to the top, clean."

"Where'd ye get such paddlewack ideas, boy?"

Not so paddlewack, considering the icy pitcher the native had left in our sleeping quarters. When I'd asked how they managed such sweet, clear water in their smoky houses, he'd explained about the boiling.

And then, as though I'd conjured her, Sacahocan spoke outside the sick house:

"The medicine boy, can you take me to him?"

Bones had guard duty, and he whistled for me. Whitman scowled as I rolled my sleeves down and went to see what Sacahocan wanted of me.

I had one foot out of the sick house when Quangatarask leaped into my arms and plastered himself to me like a poultice.

"He talks about you from dawn to dusk," Sacahocan said.

I stroked the boy's hair. "Tell me some words I can say to him."

She sang some nonsense syllables, which I repeated, and the boy smiled broadly.

"What did I sing him?"

She struggled to translate: "You are a clever hunter. Your people's young will tell of your bravery for one hundred seasons."

Quangatarask sang the song over and over while Sacahocan and I talked. Our warm breath puffed and turned to crystals between us.

"How is it that you speak English, while I barely know a word in your language?"

"A teacher," she said, dismissing the subject with a shrug.

Who, since we were the only English on these shores? Then I remembered the blond boy I'd seen streaking through the dawn. Did Sacahocan know him?

She offered me mysterious roots and leaves. "I am told your people are burning with fever. Boil these leaves three times. Twice throw the water on your plantings." She looked around. No plantings in sight. Did she think us useless or just lazy? "The third boiling, give it to your sick to drink. They'll cool by sunrise."

Warily, I took the leaves. Were they a trick? Poison? I resolved to try them on a patient or two when

Master Whitman had gone to the privy. There was little to lose; they'd all die otherwise.

It worked! We didn't lose a single man to the fever that week. Whitman crowed like a rooster, when truly it was Indian magic that had done it—and me, Elias Ridpath. Who would believe such a thing back in London?

Chapter Seven

Captain Newport's supply ship was due any day, and there was a rumor that women were aboard. Our men began sprucing themselves up to greet the ladies. The new church was finished, in case anyone would be marrying. In fact, Mr. Laydon expected his bride on the transport, and you'd think he was dancing before the gates of heaven!

We sat around the night fire telling stories. It tickled me to see my friend Bones blush like a girl at the bawdy songs. Hope soared as we waited for the good ship *Mary and Margaret*, loaded with food, medicine, weapons, new workers, and, of course, the ladies.

"Young Elias, does ya know any ditties?" asked George.

"Only girls' songs, sir," for my sisters were always trilling about flowers blooming in country gardens and babies bundled in flannel. "Nothing you'd care to hear." Then I thought of Sacahocan's song and sang the words as best as I could.

"What's it mean?" Bones asked, dancing a twig in the fire.

Oh, for a chunk of mouthwatering mutton at the end of that stick! "It means you're a clever hunter and your people's young will sing of your bravery for one hundred seasons." I glanced across the fire at Captain Smith, who threw me a look I couldn't read. Maybe he was jealous that I knew some Indian words he didn't. Hah!

Two ladies stepped off the ship. The men were disheartened to see that Mistress Forrest had come with a husband and Anne Burras was intended for Mr. Laydon, our best carpenter. We'd get no work out of *him* for awhile!

Along with the paltry supplies and disappointing number of women came orders from King James: Chief Powhatan was to be crowned an English prince! Well, I'd been in the great chief's house, where he reigned supreme with his hundred wives and as many servants and food enough for the entire English navy. Not likely that he'd be willing to wear a British crown as an underling of our king. But who was I to doubt King James himself?

Captain Smith bristled at the orders. I put my ear to every argument I could about the matter, even spying outside the window as he and Captain Newport went head-to-head like a pair of horned bucks.

"Preposterous, the very idea, Newport. James has

never been in this chief's presence. Powhatan's got ego enough to blow a strong man to the earth beneath his feet. We mustn't insult him by asking him to wear a British crown."

"Insult, John? It is an honor for him to become a tributary prince to our king. In time he'll come around."

Captain Smith slammed his hand down on his desk. "This man is not a mere *weroance*, no underchief, mind. He reigns over thirty sovereign nations of savages. He's emperor of the Tsenacommacah Empire, which, I remind you, is not overjoyed to have us swarming its shores."

I heard a shattering of glass. One of them had thrown a tumbler against the wall.

"Splendid, Newport. We have few enough of those niceties left. Soon we'll be drinking out of our boots. Your so-called supply ship brought scant goods to ease our rugged lives, so loaded was it with gifts for the *prince*. I tell you, if you so much as suggest this coronation to Powhatan, you'll see war, mark my words, blood-soaked war."

"And you the general of our army. Say no more. Powhatan must be brought to his knees."

A snort came from Captain Smith. "You delude yourself that we can simply crook our fingers and beckon an emperor such as he to come our way, dragging 14,000 illiterate, whooping savages behind him. Shh. Someone's outside."

Horror to pay if I was found spying! I scurried away, with the ideas—coronation, war—singeing the corners of my mind all afternoon at the sick house.

Life was never dull here in this foreign land, yet not so foreign. With a wave of surprise, I realized that I now thought of myself as more Virginian and less English. When had things turned?

All but a few scraps aboard Captain Newport's supply ship had spoiled. And us nearly out of what we'd traded for, with a hundred more mouths to feed. One night I found myself beside Captain Smith at the fire. "Captain, sir, it's a wonder we go hungry when there's fish and fowl all around. Also, nothing grows for us, while the Indians' storehouses overflow with food."

"Listen, boy, for I will not repeat this. There are deer in the woods and fish in the streams and fowl in abundance in their seasons, but we've no skill at hunting. Our men are afraid to chance into the forests to shoot animals three times their weight. Further, savages lurk in the forests, ready to hunt us down as though Englishmen were mere beasts. Our fishnets rot in the water. The salty marsh does not yield itself to hearty crops, and few among us are farmers. We have no choice but to trade with the Indians."

"Yes, sir, but you said the Powhatan would no longer trade with us. And after you sent them twenty muskets. They're not trustworthy men, sir."

The fire crackled, and the rest of the men had settled into low hums of dreams and longing. Captain Smith shifted beside me, raising dust with a stick.

"You never sent them the guns, sir?"

"Think. Why would I arm the enemy?"

My father's words echoed in my head and tumbled from my mouth: "An Englishman's word is his bond, sir."

"You're a naïve lad, Elias." He rose gracefully and disappeared into the darkness, leaving me flushed with embarrassment—or was it rage?

Naïve? Oh, I'd learned plenty that night, starting with this: Captain John Smith was not a man of honor.

His word was as worthless as potato eyes.

Chapter Eight

Food, that's all we talked about. Our comfort was the swine blissfully breeding on an island we'd dubbed Hog Isle. When we got desperate during the winter, we'd dispatch someone to bring back a fattened hog to sustain us. Just thinking about the juice dripping down my chin from those meaty chops was enough to keep me going another day that we were rationed a half can of ground corn each.

Bones woke me when Master Whitman was attending to a man with a scrofulous foot that we'd no doubt amputate before the week was out. My first.

"Elias, come," Bones whispered. "There's hidden food. Corn, whole lots of it, for the taking. Came over with Captain Newport's shipment. George heard them talking about it, the two captains were." Outside, he whistled for George.

Our stomachs growled all the way into the night forest to a wooden cask hidden under loamy leaves. Bones banged a scuppet, used for digging trenches, against the lock of the chest.

"You'll wake the dead throttling the thing that way," George growled.

"It's like the captain says, you've got to plant if you want to reap," said Bones, clanging away until the latch gave. You'd think that chest held the king's ransom in gold! My mouth watered as Bones lifted the lid.

A thousand brown rats scurried inside, fat and frisky from eating their way through our corn. I shrank away from the disgusting horde.

George cursed like a drunken sailor, while Bones, grinning, dangled one of the creatures by the tail. "Wouldn't taste half bad fried up with potatoes, eh, Elias?"

Before the Starving Time was over, we ate worse.

I began foraging in the woods for fleshy insects, nuts and berries, roots, herbs, acorns—anything to fill the maw of our bellies.

Sometimes I encountered Sacahocan in the forest. We spoke little as she guided my hands away from poisonous flowers and mushrooms. She said, "You are like my father, greedy for anything the earth offers."

"Hungry, is more like it."

Once as we squatted beside a hillock of wilted wildflowers, I summoned the courage to ask, "Sacahocan, have you ever seen a boy running through the woods. Someone fair skinned like me but dressed like your people?"

Abruptly, she leaped to her feet. "Never!" she said,

but I knew she had seen him, sure as I had. Why would she lie to me?

One morning while Captain Smith and Bentley were upriver scouting a fertile site for some of our colonists, I woke to the aroma of roasting meat. Outside my tent I found Mistress Forrest overseeing a fire and the turning of a spit run through a huge carcass. Someone'd shot a deer! A pan below captured its juices to baste the browning flesh.

Through the day we all turned the spit and drooled, begrudging every inch that the meat shrank as it cooked. When no one was around, I borrowed one of Master Whitman's medical cups and scooped juice from the pan. Drank it like sweet milk right from a cow. Pure heaven.

For a change we didn't complain about the fading warmth from the autumn sun because, come supper, we'd eat hot meat, like royalty.

Tender and juicy, it was. I'd never tasted meat so lip-licking savory as that succulent venison.

We all slept past sunrise the next morning, rolling luxuriously on full bellies. When I sauntered out of the tent, there stood Mistress Forrest tending the fire again.

"Stew from last night's pickings," she said. "I tossed

in the mushrooms and herbs you harvested, son. Smell it."

I hung over that kettle and sucked in the aroma that wafted in its heady steam. "Ohh!"

"As the saying goes, son, 'Hunger is the best sauce.'"

Here came Captain Smith and the others back from reconnaisance, sloshing a bucket of oysters with the shells still clicking.

Bentley headed for the stables, no doubt to kiss his prized mare. Next thing, he tore around the corner, shrieking like a she devil. "Those gawd-forsaken savages made off with my horse. By gawd, I'll kill the horse thief that stole my Buttercup, I will!"

Several men rushed to the stables. "Pity his horse is gone," I said, suddenly shy alone with Mistress Forrest.

"Gone but to a higher purpose." She knocked on the kettle, which sent back a triumphant ring.

So!

Captain Newport rehearsed us for the coronation as if we were staging a drama at Mr. Shakespeare's Globe Theatre. Meanwhile, hunger raged on. I'd stopped counting how many withered and died of starvation or the pox. We buried them three to an unmarked grave so that the Indians wouldn't know how few of us remained. We'd be easy pickings for them indeed if Chief Powhatan saw fit to attack over the coronation business.

We heard that fish were jumping farther south in Chesapeake Bay. Captain Smith organized a fishing trip while our men still had energy to cast a line and, Lord save, reel in a sturgeon half the size of our shallop.

"I am taking the best fishermen among us, which is to say four men still breathing. I shall man the boat, and you, Elias, shall mend our bodies should we fall victim to savage arrows or other ailments in the wilds."

The captain had taken a fancy to me. I suppose it was the copper hair. Maybe he saw in me the boy he'd once been or the boy who'd one day be his son. Though I sorely missed my own father, Captain Smith was a poor substitute. He'd shown himself to be less than honorable and arrogant besides. I didn't like the man one whit.

Still, I had little choice but to climb aboard the shallop when he ordered me to do so.

What adventures lay ahead? What dangers?

Chapter Nine

We had but to wade into the shallow shoreline of the Chesapeake and scoop fish into our arms until their tails stopped flapping. Mr. Mooney chomped into a fish, sucking the raw meat and spitting out the scales and bones. The rest of us preferred to fry and eat our catch without the eyes staring back at us.

Heading home, our boat loaded and our bodies stinking of the salt sea, Captain Smith saw a large tail flip up over yonder. Wading out, he said, "Can't hurt to have one more fish as a bonus catch—yeowwww!"

I'd never heard a yell like this from man or beast. I dived in to see what had caused such an outcry. A strange creature swam past me, wide and flat, flapping water wings and whipping a long, pointed tail. On its underside three eyelike holes sucked in water.

Stingrays. Venomous. I'd heard talk of such.

Captain Smith bellowed, pumping his hand up out of the water. "My wrist is stung. I am doomed to a wretched, painful death. Ahhhhh!"

I slipped my shoulder under his good arm and hauled him back to shore, kicking madly. He weighed at least twice as much as me. The others took him from my arms while I caught my breath. The wound gaped horribly, jagged and bleeding with a spiny needle sticking out.

The captain's arm swelled as if someone blew air into it. I watched the pain ripple up the arm to his shoulder like a worm crawling under his skin.

"Nobody survives a stingray attack," John Mooney said. "Nobody."

The captain wailed like a baby and between gasps said, "Three wars I've fought and never been in greater agony. Ahhhh! Mooney, Rysdale, dig my grave, for I'm dying, and let it be sooner rather than later."

There being no shovel, the men began scrabbling at the dirt with sticks and bare hands and drinking cups, fear blazing in their eyes.

What did the Indians do for stingray poison? *What to do?* Then an odd peace washed over me, and my mind began to click away at what I must do first, second, third. That stinger had to come out. The pliers in my bag made that job easy, but what next? Press the wound together to stop the bleeding so the jagged edges could begin to heal.

Sweat poured down the captain's face and pooled at his neck. He turned white, then green, rolling himself over to retch again and again.

I remembered how the icy water had soothed Mr. Bentley's mouth, and I motioned for Mr. Mooney to fetch me a bucket of cold bay water. But when I plunged the captain's arm into the bucket, he howled like a hound baying at the moon.

Heat, then. Master Whitman had mentioned boiling oil to heal wounds. Water would have to do but not boiling so as to raise blisters on the captain's arm.

"Mr. Rysdale, set this bucket of water over the fire." Ordering grown men around boosted my confidence. They gladly took my orders too, terrified as Captain Smith begged for a quick and merciful death.

I refused him that. "No, sir, I shall not allow you to die."

Mr. Rysdale brought the water. "Prop the captain up. Sir, I'm going to plunge your arm into this water. It's hot, to be sure. It'll relieve the pain." *I hoped.*

He nodded weakly, his face the color of seawater. Mooney and Rysdale continued digging the grave while the other two men attended to the shallop and its prized catch, which would feed so many in the fort.

Within minutes the pain eased. "Heat more water!" I shouted, holding Captain Smith's arm firmly in the bucket. We kept pouring off cold, adding hot.

Hours passed, the grave grew deeper, and still I sat with the captain. Every time I lifted his arm out of the hot water, the pain flooded back. Once he fainted, and I let him be, still holding his arm in the water until aching muscles pulled taut across my back. Now Rysdale was waist deep in the hole.

If I dozed, I woke when the water cooled and the captain cried out. Once I startled myself awake—or I might have been dreaming—when I saw a grayish-white something flapping at the tip of Mr. Mooney's sword. A stingray? And then, maybe four hours into the ordeal, I lifted the arm out to add more hot water, and Captain Smith said, "It's over. I've lived through it."

Rysdale gratefully leaped out of the grave. I lay the captain down on the ground and covered him with a thin blanket. I shivered beside him all night, often with my ear to his chest to be sure he was breathing.

In the morning it was stingray steak for breakfast. The meat was sinewy and salty but quite satisfying.

Captain Smith declined his portion.

"I am beholden to you, lad," the captain said as we neared Jamestown.

What a curious feeling to have a man owe you his life. I didn't like it. Such a debt was huge, and how could—or should—it ever be paid? And what if you'd saved someone's life, but you didn't admire him any more afterward than before?

Captain Smith, more than pleased with himself, had his own method of settling the debt. "From this day forward I shall take you with me on every expedition. You'll experience wonders no lad has ever encountered. And I shall have my personal physician at my side." He jabbed me in the ribs as our shallop glided through the waters.

"Yes, sir," I said solemnly.

Chapter Ten

Captain Smith had never been defeated in any battle until this one: his rival, Captain Newport, would be taking 120 of us to the coronation, and Captain Smith would not be among us. It was a blow to his ego, indeed, but I secretly gloated at his humbling.

Master Whitman was fallen with a walloping cough that shook the very walls of our tent. Struggling to hold his head up, he prepared me for the trip to Werowocomoco.

"Ye'll have ten dozen fragile souls to care for, lad, on this foolhardy adventure." A fit of coughing overcame him.

It hurt my chest to see him hacking away so. "Here, sir, let this soothe your throat and lungs." I gave him a cup of Sacahocan's snakeroot and sassafras brew.

His face screwed up. "Bah! What's in it?"

"It's a simple." *Simple* was any single English herb used for medicinal purposes. "Captain Newport brought clippings of betony and toadflax for us."

"Feels very smooth going down," he conceded, dropping his head to his pillow. "Now, lad, ye must pack a full bag of medical supplies. Ye won't get off as easily as with the stingray disaster." Cough-cough. Another gulp of Sacahocan's tea. "Remember what I showed ye about the cups? Light a small flame inside to create a vacuum. Apply them aptly to a man's back, and they'll suck the poisons right to the surface. For muscle pains, mind, and deep internal wounds. In a dire case combine the cupping with bloodletting, lest ye lose the patient."

"Yes, sir." It cost me nothing to say it, and it pleased him.

Though Captain Newport truly hadn't supplied us with English herbs, he had brought over colonies of leeches. Seeing them squirm and swish their blood-sucking black bodies in the jar made my skin crawl. Now Master Whitman was reaching for the jar, shaking it until the creepies inside tumbled dizzily.

"Review the humors and vapors, lad. Very important. And should ye have to lop off a limb, use these pretty leeches to stem the hemorrhaging. Keep them hungry, boy, but tease them with a drop of blood, yer own if ye must, to prime their pumps. Then leave them to their business. They'll suck up five times their body weight in blood." He was seized with another coughing fit, and I rescued the leech jar from his hands.

When he quieted again, he said, "Remember all I've taught ye. No paddlewack, boy, swear it."

"Sir, you need your rest." I gently closed his

eyelids. "I'll leave the tea here beside you." His chest rattled and whistled as he drifted into a deep sleep. I slipped away to make ready for the trip, for we'd be an army marching on foot all the way into Powhatan territory.

Captain Newport had sent lavish gifts ahead to soften up the chief. Three barges groaned their way upriver under the burden of a huge canopy bed, diverse fancy chests and chairs, a scarlet cloak befitting a prince, and lumber and glass to be assembled into a proper cottage of the lush English countryside. Myself, a lad of the London streets, had never seen such, and here soon natives in far-off Virginia would boast of this remarkable dwelling—if Chief Powhatan didn't kill us all first.

At sunrise we clattered and clanged our way into Werowocomoco, with its odd thatched lean-tos. The chief's warriors awaited us, bows at their sides. Captain Newport stood on the stump of a tree and unfurled a vellum proclamation. Its main thrust was that we'd come in peace, in the name of King James, to honor their chief with a British crown in elaborate ceremonies to commence first thing tomorrow.

Throughout the night natives arrived from all corners and tribes of the Powhatan Empire. Though we were a sizable crew, we were greatly outnumbered. If each Indian had a bow and a half-dozen arrows, we were doomed to shed barrels of English blood. A billion of Master Whitman's leeches could not save us!

The day dawned bright and warm. Natives wearing paint and feathers, a bit of buckskin, and not much else rose all around us. We left our gear near our beds, as did they. This was to be a day of trust, of peace. We marched through dense evergreen forests toward the chief's house, easy to spot from a distance because of its sprawl, with the smoke billowing out of the hole in its roof.

The house was filled to bursting. Someone led us through the throng to the feet of the chief. We sat in a half circle, facing him, with a row of women behind us. Priestesses, medicine women, I guessed.

Thick smoke clouded the dark house. Someone tapped me on the shoulder. I spun about and recognized Sacahocan. I was set to jump to my feet until she whispered,

"Stay, unless Chief Powhatan tells us to rise."

"Where is Quangatarask?"

"Children do not come here. Quiet."

Someone threw water on the cairn surrounding the fire in the center of the room. The stones sizzled like oil in a pan. A wave of fresh steam rose at my back. The steady drumming and chanting from the south wall lulled me until my eyelids grew heavy and my heart throbbed to the rhythm of their drums.

Captain Newport rose and unfurled the scarlet cloak. "Wahunsenacah, chief of the Powhatan Empire, I present you with this royal cloak from King James VI of Scotland, the selfsame King James I of England, sovereign liege of all of Great Britain."

Ask me, and I'd say Captain Newport was trying to impress Chief Powhatan, but I could read the chief's scoffing: *Scotland? England? Bah. I am emperor of the Appamatuck, the Kecoughtan, the Nansemond, the Mataponi, the Pamunkee, the Rappahannock, and a score of other nations. What are two little backward island countries compared to my vast empire?*

So, when Captain Newport tried to drape the cloak over the chief's shoulders, the drumming stopped, and a gasp rose from the Indians, shocked by this breach of conduct. The chief shrugged off the offending cloak, and his voice thundered through the ceremonial house. "Where is Nantaquod?"

I watched the knot in Captain Newport's throat ripple. "Nantaquod, Chief Powhatan?"

"Yes, yes, the one with the copper head. Why is he not here? And where are the fire sticks he promised me?"

Captain Newport looked puzzled, but I knew that the chief had given the name of Nantaquod to one of our own. I tugged at Newport's coat. "Sir, he means Captain Smith."

"Smith promised him guns?" Captain Newport hissed toward me and then turned to the chief with a broad smile. "Ah, yes! I'm afraid Captain Smith had pressing tasks at our camp, Chief Powhatan. He'll make good on his promises in due time. See? Our party is one hundred and twenty strong. Is one man's absence so noticeable?" He sputtered a nervous laugh. I saw his annoyance over his rival's treacherous promise of guns.

"Then bring me Nantaquod's son!" the chief shouted. His eyes scanned our group. "You, boy. Rise."

Me?

Me!

Chapter Eleven

I staggered to my feet, swallowing a plum-sized lump.

"Copperhead, son of Nantaquod. Come." He jerked me to a spot to the right of him so that our bodies made an L shape. A charge raced through me at his touch, much like a whip to a horse's back. I stood close enough to count the shells around his neck, the hairs on his chin.

"Copperhead is the youngest of the men here," he said.

Man? My pride swelled, if not my courage.

"Bring me the youngest woman. An old warrior enjoys the comfort of the young."

Sacahocan positioned herself on the other side of Chief Powhatan, facing me. Watching her closely, I prayed that I wouldn't do anything stupid to annoy the chief, but what was the smart thing to do? If there was a signal in Sacahocan's strange pale eyes, I couldn't read it.

A woman rushed forward with a bowl of wash water and feathers to dry our hands.

Chief Powhatan pressed a ringed finger on each of our shoulders, Sacahocan's and mine, shouting to the hundreds of people assembled, "Now I stand ready to become an English prince!"

The ceremony began with a bugle blast from Master Wainright. Captain Newport proclaimed "in the name of the king" and so forth, followed by rounds of "Huzza, huzza!" from our men. Then the chief stood on a footstool to make an even longer speech in his language, shells and bangles clickety-clacking as he waved his hands. Not to be outdone, Newport climbed onto a higher bench and offered a still puffier speech. The *huzza huzzas* were growing less enthusiastic among our own, and the natives fidgeted around restlessly. I smelled a growing anger, pungent as overripe peaches.

Sacahocan and I exchanged glances. We both saw that our leaders were trying to outshine one another.

Captain Newport uncloaked a tall cross, which he jammed into the earth at the chief's feet. "Observe, sir, the two arms of this humble rood represent you and my king, herein inscribed as Jacobus Rex."

The chief bristled. "Jacobus Rex or King James, which?"

"Ah, just as you are called both Wahunsenacah and Powhatan, so is my king known by two names."

The chief smoothed his hands over the wood, and Captain Newport rushed to explain further.

"Here, where the two arms meet and are knotted? This symbolizes the joining of our two worthy peoples as one."

Now, I'd never been a church mouse, but even I knew that this cross meant something else entirely. No one protested, not even the Reverend Mr. Storch. Someone translated, and natives around us murmured—approval or threats? No telling.

Nearly an hour slogged by with more speeches. I shifted left and right, my toes folded inside the boots that refused to grow with my feet. Sacahocan stood as still as a statue.

Smoke clouded my eyes, peppered my throat, and I resisted coughing during Chief Powhatan's latest speech. At last, the dribbling stream of words ended, and Newport unveiled the splendid copper crown. Powhatan's eyes lit up with glee.

I knew the purpose of this crown; I'd eavesdropped on the arguments between our two captains, and we underlings had talked into the night about the meaning of the whole mock coronation. Once the crown rested on the chief's head, he'd be a British subject. Though he might not guess what this would augur for his people, we understood that his land, his entire empire, would belong to King James, and he, Powhatan, would be just a governor on a distant shore. King James fully expected the diverse tribes of the Powhatan Empire to become Christians and behave like civilized English.

George had explained the plan to Bones and me, scoffing, "T'won't work. Savages as proper Englishmen? Might as well try to convert trash-bin pickings into gold bricks."

I shot a glance toward Sacahocan. Did she guess the truth?

Chief Powhatan reached out to accept the glittering copper treasure. Bad turn: Captain Newport meant to set the crown on the chief's head, not in his hands, but Chief Powhatan wouldn't lower his head or kneel to receive it. Captain Newport was a squat man, and the chief towered a full head and shoulders over him. The captain knelt and bowed his head to demonstrate the proper way to accept a crown, but Powhatan refused to bow to a foreigner.

Panting and wheezing, Newport spent himself by kneeling again and again, demonstrating the proper demeanor for one being dubbed with royalty. I saw amusement flicker across Sacahocan's face. A few titters of embarrassed laughter echoed through the room. None of us English had ever been to a coronation, but we knew how it was supposed to go, and this one wasn't going well. A low chant, like bees buzzing, rose from the throats of the natives. The air grew tense, not to mention dense with the heady aroma of burning tobacco. Ten more minutes, and I'd swoon. No! For once I knew what was best. I stepped forward, hand trembling. "Chief Powhatan, sir?" I said timidly.

Sacahocan shot me a warning, but I didn't heed it.

"May I, honorable Chief Powhatan?" On tiptoes I snaked my hand past the long tail of hair that hung over the chief's left ear. Newport seized the moment to place the crown askew on the chief's lowered head, even as the attendant pinned my arms behind my back. George leaped to his feet to rescue me, but then the chief raised his head, straightened the crown, and grinned like a jester. All was forgiven, and a huge sigh of relief filled the room. As though our hearts had been stopped, now the drummers began our heartbeats again, and the chanters resumed their hypnotizing melodies. My arms were released, and I hugged the aching bones of my shoulders.

On Newport's signal, one of our men lobbed a shot outside the house to alert our ship offshore where a falconet waited to fire. Chief Powhatan jumped at the rumble of cannon fire, which Newport quickly explained was our way of proclaiming this a grand and glorious day for both our peoples.

The Indians had mere drummers and singers; we had cannon fire. Never was I so proud to be an Englishman.

Powhatan women of many tribes laid out a

steaming feast before us. We dug in with wooden spoons and small paddles. Wahunsenacah, prince of Great Britain, himself handed me a fat turkey leg. "Enjoy, Copperhead," he said, shoving it toward my eager mouth, and since it was an order from a royal prince of England, I sank my teeth into the juicy meat.

Then, with my belly filled beyond its happiest dreams, I looked around for Sacahocan, to see if she liked how I'd gotten the whole ceremony out of trouble. She was gone without so much as a wave. And us now kinsmen—or so I thought.

Powhatan thought otherwise, which we were to discover within a fortnight.

Chapter Twelve

The thick haze of mosquitoes had finally died off with winter's blast. Back in Jamestown, Captain Smith champed to hear about the coronation.

"Chief Powhatan asked for you, sir. Scores of us, and he noticed you not there."

"He did, did he?" A smile spread under his mustache, which he curled at the tips with spit on his fingers. "And I'm told that you saved the whole mortifying ceremony with your quick thinking."

"No, sir. I only moved things along. Captain Newport was near collapsing."

"Yes, tell me again of Newport's bumbling about."

I embellished the story each time through. His mustache shook with laughter until Captain Newport came around the bend.

"Well, Christopher," Captain Smith said. "I've been hearing of your triumph at Werowocomoco."

Master Whitman asked nothing about the doings at the coronation, other than to inquire as to whether I'd had to wield the lancet.

"My services weren't needed, sir. Not even to remove a sliver."

"Just as well, since ye left behind the leeches. That

was risky, boy," he grumbled, but he could say little because he'd made scant recovery from his cough. Still, he dragged himself out each morning to attend to men in the sick house.

Those up and about had found a pile of box turtles in hibernation, and every fire blazed under a pot of turtle soup or stew. The shells tottered on their rounded backs, drying in the thin sunlight before they found new life as bowls and baskets. As Mistress Forrest said, "Waste not, want not."

The turtles no doubt *wanted* a fate other than what we offered.

Once they were eaten, along with the fish we'd brought back, we faced a lean winter ahead. Our only comfort was the swine thriving on Hog Isle.

"Those hogs are our ace in the hole," said George, a gambling man who'd made a fortune twice over—and lost twice as much. "Aye, Bones, do you think about those piggies living the high life over on that island?"

Bones chuckled. "Gentlemen having their way with the ladies—"

"And all of 'em fattening up for our Sunday supper, come February."

Meanwhile we were eating slugs and barley gruel.

"We've no choice but to trade with the savages

again," said Captain Smith when snow snuffed out the last of our puny wheat crop.

"But sir," I protested. All I had to do was raise my eyebrows to remind him of his broken promise to Chief Powhatan. And it wasn't his worst, I'd learned from George. Once before Chief Powhatan had asked the captain how long the English meant to stay on the shores of the New World.

"Only so long as it takes to escape Spanish invaders who are sailing in this direction," he'd told the chief. The answer sat well, for the Indians also despised the Spanish. What Captain Smith didn't say was that by order of King James we were to to stay in Virginia and expand beyond our small fort. In short, take over much of Powhatan's land.

"You mean to trade with the Powhatan, sir?"

"Closer to home are the Pamunkee."

Sacahocan's tribe.

"Tomorrow we shall load our barge with the beads and copper and worthless trinkets they treasure, and we'll return with bushels enough to sustain us through the winter. Prepare for the voyage upriver, men." He nodded toward me. "You, too, of course, lad."

What an amazing spy network the Pamunkee had! Late that afternoon Sacahocan and Quangatarask arrived, laden with corn and smoked sturgeon. Mistress Forrest and Mistress Laydon rushed forward with blankets to cover the two Indians. This I saw because Master Whitman and I were barbering outside our tent. My artistry left Mr. Mooney with oily porcupine spikes, for I was turning out to be a better surgeon than a barber.

Quangatarask presented his dark-moon head to me for cutting. I laced my fingers through his hair. English hair grew coarser, curlier, and dirtier. How did those Indians stay so clean? I pretended to snip at the hair, and the clip-clip of the scissors satisfied him. Sacahocan looked on. Embarrassed, I introduced her to Master Whitman.

"Sir, this is the girl who brought the herbs and roots I showed you."

"Bah, paddlewack, that!" Whitman said, chopping away at Master Wainright's woolly locks between fits of coughing.

Sacahocan said, "Ly-iss, I must talk with you."

We wandered over to the stables. Quangatarask stood on a stool peering into the dark, charmed by the horses, while Sacahocan and I talked.

"Strange new sickness comes to my people. Fevers with red, itchy bumps. Our people die. I have nothing for it."

"Pox, measles. Yes, we see those all the time." And then it hit me. We English brought those dread diseases to the New World! That was as barbaric as burning their villages—slow, cruel death rather than flames.

Sacahocan drew a handful of herbs and roots from the leather pouch around her neck. "Here, for the sickness that comes from our land, and you will give me medicines for the sickness that comes from *your* land?"

"Wait here." I dashed back to the tent, grabbing one of the turtle shells on the way, which I filled with half a dozen bottles of Master Whitman's tonic, aqua vitae, gum of spearmint, and unguent. Handing this traveling apothecary to her, I said, "This one is to drink, this to clean the skin, this to smear on the itchy-scratchies. The fever rages for two or three days, but around half recover, especially if they're well fed and drink sweet water and are otherwise healthy." Our men, of course, were not.

She listened, memorizing what to do with each vial.

"Master Whitman says—"

"Who is Master Whitman?"

How to explain *apprentice* and *master?* "He's the medicine man I learn from. He says fever comes from too much bad blood. It must be let out before the patient can get better. Cutting," I said, with a shudder.

Sacahocan's brow wrinkled in puzzlement. "I do not think so. My people teach that we are sick when our lives are not in . . . " She couldn't find the word, but she showed me both palms up, rising and falling, like measuring weights.

"Balance?"

"Yes, in *balance* with the animals, also trees and air and spirits that light the path we walk. To make the sickness go away, I must help them put their days back in . . . I forget the word, so long since I have used it. Yes, now it comes, in *har-mo-nee* with nature." She held up the turtle shell filled with my vials, as if she was offering it to God or to her gods. "I will use my medicine and yours, together."

"I, too." The idea sent ripples of excitement through me, which none of Whitman's teachings had. He'd call it paddlewack. I'd have to bring this notion out of the secret chambers of my mind when I treated patients struck down with fevers and all manner of mysterious aches.

And then we got into a spirited discussion about stingray poisoning.

"Very hot water? I never knew!" she said, full of admiration.

"It eases the pain and draws out the poison." We

were two physicians consulting on cases. Who would believe it?

Quangatarask hung over the half door of the stable, mimicking the horses' high-pitched whinnies. The blanket had slid off his back, revealing a plump brown bottom indifferent to the cold. Sacahocan smiled shyly.

And then the mood shifted. "Ly-iss, I have heard that your people come to my village to trade for food."

"Yes, tomorrow."

"Tell your chief. Do not come. There is . . . danger."

I laughed. "I have no say in what happens, Sacahocan."

"You must warn them. You are their medicine man. They will listen to you!"

She had such faith in me, and yet I had to tell her, "The truth is, I have as much power around here as a box turtle."

Chapter Thirteen

The clouds hung heavy, itching to drop the first snow. My ears stung with cold.

George and Bones tried to cheer me with riddles before our departure for Pamunkee territory.

Chin propped on a rusty shovel, George posed, "Whot kind of room's not in a house a'tall? Tell him, Bones."

Bones jammed his shovel into the hardened snow and twisted his lips to stave off the laughter bubbling in him. "A MUSH-room, Elias. A mushroom!"

I smiled, but my spirit was lower than river silt. In an hour I'd be on a shallop, wending our way to Pamunkee territory. I'd told Captain Smith about Sacahocan's warning. He'd swatted away my worry like a pesty mosquito.

The ankle-deep snow seemed to shrink my boots into vises, clamping on my frozen toes.

George saw me grimace. "All right, a jolly one. When's a boy like a bear?"

"When he's BARE-foot," I snapped, wishing I was.

Captain Smith came around. "Mr. Tyding, young Bones, enjoying a workman's holiday, are you?"

Bones said, "Yes, *sir!*"

The captain thrust the shovel into Bones's hands. "Dig a hole before the fort's buried in snow."

Bones and George began stabbing their shovels into the hard earth, with George muttering, "Can't even eat snake in the winter. The slitheries have got the good sense to go into hiding when it gets this nippy. You and I'd have done well to follow. Ach, me back."

Captain Smith stepped into a pile of banked earth, deliberately scattering it. "Mr. Tyding, you're coming with me. Look sharp. Young Bones, keep shoveling. Pretend it's coal for the heaters we don't have. And you, Elias, ready for an adventure? Medical supplies in hand, do you?"

"Yes, sir," I replied with a sigh, as Bones strutted behind Captain Smith with the shovel over his shoulder like a musket, mouthing *mushroom, Elias, mushroom*.

Aboard one of our three barges, the captain announced, "We go first to the Nansemond to see what food stores we can bleed from them."

At the Nansemond village Captain Smith demanded the absurd sum of 400 baskets of corn, which the *weroance* could not give, short of starving his own people. Under extreme pressure, he revealed that Chief Powhatan had ordered all of the tribes in his empire not to trade with us.

"Flexing his muscle now that he's a prince?" Enraged, Captain Smith fired his musket into the air, and when that didn't scatter the Indians, he set fire to one of their houses. The brittle thatch popped and sizzled and then burst into leaping flames. An old woman stepped out of her house with a baby sitting on each hip, her eyes blazing with the rage that reflected my own.

"The rest of the village goes up in flames if you don't hand over the food," Captain Smith shouted. People shot like cannon fire out to the storehouse. When our barge was heavy with ill-gotten corn, we sailed upriver until the smoke was only a black dot in the sky.

Would Captain Smith use the same cruel tactics against the Pamunkee? How could a hero of his stature have sunk to such mercenary lows? I remembered my father saying, "Hunger makes wolves of men."

He dozed on the deck under a deerskin mantle from a different trading mission. How had he extorted that piece of goods? Me, I shivered in my thin coat that no longer buttoned and holey gloves that left my fingers at the mercy of the falling temperature.

My feet swelled in their boots like yeasted dough. Everything hurt, and an ache deep within hurt most, the kind that grows like thistle, prickly and ugly and good for nothing.

The captain woke from his peaceful sleep. “Successful mission,” he said, yawning.

Anger roiled in me. “You will *not* set the Pamunkee village on fire!” I shouted.

“Watch yer mouth, lad,” warned George.

“No! You’re an evil man, Captain. The Nansemond did nothing to hurt us. They only meant to keep their own people from starving, and the Pamunkee girl has been generous to us—food and herbs for our sick. Don’t you dare destroy them!”

I expected a sharp crack on my cheek, but the captain rolled his shoulders in callous indifference. “I’ll let your insolence pass, young Elias, because it’s Christmas.”

Christmas? I’d lost track entirely. Longing sapped me of my anger and pierced me deeper than the cold. What sort of Christmas would my family have? A hot plum pudding, stretched among the four of them? A lavender handkerchief for our mother maybe, a bottle of ink for Catherine, our poet, and hair ribbons for Mary and Isobel? I wished I could give them such wondrous gifts. Would they think of me, so far off, on this holiday, or was mine a name rarely mentioned, like our father's?

We spent Christmas Eve in the Kecoughtan village, warming our innards with blackberry wine. The Indians knew nothing of our Lord, but they knew how to celebrate. Still rankled by the Nansemond massacre, I steered clear of the captain, smoking my first tobacco pipe—and my last, if I had any say in it. The Kecoughtans fed us well and invited us to sleep inside, near the fires. My toes stretched and defrosted, finally. On Christmas morning, our heads swimming with the wine and tobacco, we were on the river again, heavier by a few bushels of corn. And I dreaded what lay ahead in the Pamunkee village.

The captain stayed to himself, jotting endlessly in his notebook, heating and stirring the ink to keep it from icing. I can't guess how he wrapped his frozen fingers around the quill. As we neared Pamunkee land, he began shouting orders across the water to the other barges. Christmas cheer rose and vanished with his icy breath. "Wainright, Mooney, Bentley, Dobbin, remain on this barge. Wait for the booty for loading. Do not, do not go ashore to encounter these savages unless you wish to have your skin flayed with razor-sharp mollusk shells and the remaining flesh roasted like hog meat. I have seen this, and it isn't pretty."

Fear feeds the imagination. I *felt* the howling pain, the heat rendering my flesh black, my bones a brittle white.

Captain Smith noticed my stricken face. "Easy, lad. Now, George Tyding, it's well-known that you're a lazy lout—"

"Why, thank you, sir!"

"—but you're also a sharp-eyed shooter."

"With the dice, to be sure," Mr. Dobbin said.

"As well with a matchlock and pistol," Captain Smith said. "Men, should you hear Mr. Tyding's double shot, you're to rush ashore, for we will only fire if we're in dire straits. Clear, gentleman?"

"Aye, sir," came a chorus of voices from all three barges.

"So, Mr. Tyding, you and young Elias and I will row a canoe to the shore for a friendly rendezvous with our Pamunkee neighbors."

"Why me, Captain?" I squeaked, as Sacahocan's warning came rolling through my mind.

"Because you, lad, are my son. That's what the savages believe. Even *they* would not slaughter a father in the sight of his son."

Chapter Fourteen

It was too quiet when we came ashore at Menapacute. "The trees have eyes and ears," Captain Smith whispered. I hadn't a gun like the others. "Draw your surgeon's lancet if necessary," the captain ordered.

I don't think he meant for medical purposes.

Chief Opechancanough, Powhatan's brother, welcomed us like family, pushing the captain and me back-to-back to take our measure. "The son passes the father," he said merrily.

Too jolly; something was ticking. George shot me an anxious glance. I knew Captain Smith and Chief Opechancanough were like cat and dog. Earlier in the year, the chief had taken our captain hostage. Captain Smith only lived to tell the tale by confounding his captors with a compass. Whichever way it turned, the dial pointed due north. No Indian had ever seen such an astonishing gewgaw. Now Chief Opechancanough was slapping us on our backs like we were tavern mates, but he surely knew our captain would exact revenge—and soon.

Despite the waves bubbling under the surface, we sat by the fire warming our frozen pipes on a hot, tasty brew. Then came the flashing of copper trinkets and beads, needles and pins, hatchets and knives, to be bartered for belly-filling foodstuffs. The chief summoned a parade of men bearing baskets overflowing with corn and bread and dried meat.

The captain rifled through the first baskets, satisfied with goods gotten at a fair price—until he plunged his hand deep into the third and found the bottom raised so the basket held less. The fourth, likewise. He spun around to the chief. "You deceive us!" He snatched the sack of hatchets and knives out of the chief's hands. Then, like my sisters fighting over a doll, they tugged the sack back and forth. It would have been comical if a vision of seared flesh hadn't bolted through my mind.

A devilish smile pulled Chief Opechancanough's lips upward when he finally clutched the bag to his bejeweled chest. "Ten more baskets for our neighbors," he ordered. "Load the foreigners' barges."

We all chortled in joyless relief. Captain Smith crackled like parchment. You could slice the air between us. The chief left us alone for a moment—a calculated move—and George said, "The whole thing stinks as bad as a net of rotten shrimp, Captain."

"Aye. Listen. What do you hear outside?"

George said, "Thrumming. Like blood coursing through one hundred veins."

"Exactly. The savages surround the tent, dozens of them."

George lit the matchcord at both ends. Its pungent odor stung my throat as he primed to shoot his matchlock at the captain's orders.

I reached into my medical bag and wrapped my fist around my lancet.

The chief was brimming with mock cheer when he returned: "This night, honored guests, you will stay and sail off in the dawn."

What choice had we? The tide was out, our barges grounded in mud, and freezing besides. A restless night stretched ahead. The chief sent in more supper than we could possibly stuff down our gullets. Captain Smith made the Indians taste everything first. They survived and left us to one another.

I'd just closed an eye, with the lancet under my pillow, when Sacahocan ducked into our tent.

"Shh, Ly-iss, leave. Now. They watch 'til you grow drowsy with food and drink. Then they will kill you. Kill you, Ly-iss!" She gathered our bags and thrust them into our arms. "Go!"

"She's a decoy. Ignore the girl," Captain Smith said.

Sacahocan gave him a withering look. "I see the future. You are not there."

"Please, sir, trust her." My eyes darted from Sacahocan to the captain as he weighed her words. George had the gun pointed up toward the smoke billowing out of the tent.

Captain Smith gave the order: "Fire!"

George shot into the air, quickly reignited the gun, and fired again. Sacahocan jumped at the thundering sound—the signal to our men on the barges.

"You'd better get out of here," I warned her. "Our men will soon swarm the village with loads of firepower." I didn't add, *not just clumsy matchlocks; real snaphaunce guns fired by flint—and deadly.*

But the men would be marching right into an ambush.

Captain Smith motioned for us to snake our way out of the tent, below the sight of the Pamunkee surrounding us, just as Sacahocan had done. "Our only chance," he mouthed.

Dizzy with fright, I hurled my medical bag onto my back and sank to my belly between the two men. I'd regret the fire we left behind—or so I thought—but once outside, I burned with fear.

The Pamunkees towered above us as we elbowed and kneed our way through the cold, dry earth, swallowing grit. I dared not look up, but I knew there were bows drawn above us as we crept through the brush. I sent my mother and sisters a silent good-bye and clamped my tongue between my teeth, vowing not to cry out, even if I was pierced with a dozen arrows.

What were they waiting for? Was this Opechancanough's grim joke to make us slither like cowards, only to shoot us when we reached the barge, consigning us to a fiery leap into frigid waters?

Captain Smith gave the order that would surely cause us to be slaughtered like livestock. "Stand up, men." I stumbled to my unsteady feet, sure I'd totter and disgrace myself. All around me, Indian eyes gleamed in the moonlight. They seemed never to blink. Behind the row of men, Sacahocan wove her fingers at her chin. Her lips moved silently.

"Walk calmly," the captain ordered, and we filed past the Indians.

Why had they let us go? We heard the boots of our men trampling through dry brush. No armor; they'd learned from the natives about surprising the enemy. Still, the flames of so many matchcords would have given them away if crunching snow hadn't.

"Halt!" Captain Smith commanded. The small army froze. "The enemy's all around us, letting us pass for now. I suspect Opechancanough's letting us believe we've escaped unscathed, only to ambush us on our barges. Watch your backs, men."

Die now or die later. A diabolical choice that made my blood run cold.

The captain squared his shoulders. "Turn around and march like proud Englishmen toward our barges. Prepare to fire at my word."

With each step, I expected an arrow in my back. The taste of grit would be the last thing I'd know.

Chapter Fifteen

If Chief Opechancanough's battle plan was to move us like puppets and inspire sheer terror, he succeeded nobly. Jaws locked in our fierce determination not to be cowardly fools, the group of us marched silently onto our barges, surprised to find ourselves alive.

Once safely on the boat, George murmured, "Sweet Jesus, look. Our matchcords must've have set something ablaze."

Flames from the village we'd just escaped now turned the night orange. Sacahocan and Quangatarask—were they safe?

We watched the fire in the distance, counting the hours until the tide would release us from the mud. At first dawn two of our barges sailed away, but the Indians had stolen back our hard-won food when our men had gone ashore at George's signal.

Captain Smith cursed as we prepared to follow the emptied barges.

Suddenly, three Pamunkees tore out of the trees and leaped onto our boat, bellowing war cries and swinging hatchets—English hatchets. I slammed myself to the bottom of the shallop, rather to be trampled than hacked to death. Knees drawn to my chest, I rolled into the smallest possible target.

A red pool widened beside me. Blood gushed from Bentley's chest. His face was bleached of color. Sickened, I dragged the poor man into a corner. Now's when I needed Master Whitman's leeches: *They suck up five times their body weight in blood.* I put my ear to Bentley's chest, my hand to his lips. No sound, no breath. He hung in my arms, and I understood the meaning of *deadweight.*

Guns fired. A Pamunkee somersaulted backward into the water with a tunnel in his gut. A second Indian lay in the keel of the boat, with Mr. Mooney's boot at his throat. His thigh shattered, his face purple, he vainly raised his hatchet an inch off the floor before gasping his last breath.

Carnage everywhere. Mr. Stanley's head was nearly cleaved in two like firewood. Giles lay facedown, motionless. Cutperth floated belly-up in the river, already fodder for the gulls. I was a useless apprentice; even the best surgeon could not raise the dead.

And George? Where was he?

I slipped in blood sliming the floor, looking for George and Captain Smith. If George was not to come back alive, how would I ever tell Bones? All was silent. I thought myself the last alive, the last on all the earth. Loneliness coursed through me like wind through a tunnel. My teeth chattered uncontrollably.

Then from the shore Captain Smith sprang out of the trees and lunged for a tall Indian, dragging him by the tail of hair streaming down his shoulders—Chief Opechancanough! The captain shoved him toward the smoldering village.

What could I do? I jumped off the boat and followed. The air was clouded with smoke, snowing soot all around us. A dozen houses lay in heaps of wood and charred mats and skins. Surrounding trees were shrunken embers.

Captain Smith released the chief's mane and pistol prodded him into the center of the village. Frightened eyes peered out of the few houses left standing. "You savages won't understand my words. Opechancanough, order them to load ten baskets of corn onto my shallop."

The chief said nothing while his men stared in confusion. The only sound was Captain Smith cocking his pistol. "Tell them."

Chief Opechancanough barked some words, and the men scurried to refill and deliver the baskets of corn. Would Smith let the chief go when the barge was reloaded? Hadn't we done enough damage already, for in the clearing lay a circle of people on woven mats moaning with terrible burns. A medicine man and Sacahocan hurried from mat to mat. My eyes caught hers. Hatred and betrayal burned in those eyes.

I took a deep breath, opened my medical bag, and knelt beside her at the mat of a small boy with wide, frightened eyes. I knew the thin wail that called my name: "Ly-iss."

I gently dabbed a gob of Master Whitman's tallow and honey paste on Quangatarask's blackened arm. "The best for burns. Trust me."

Sacahocan jerked the jar out of my hand and tossed it into the bushes. "Trust you?" Her words were the growl of a dog.

"What else have we, with dying and burned flesh all around us?" I sprang to my feet to retrieve the bottle of burn paste, which is when I noticed a mat set apart from the others.

"George! Where are you hurt?"

He uncovered his left arm. A butcher's slice had opened it to white bone. The flesh below the wound was gray, leached of blood. I knew that Master Whitman would amputate above the gangrenous deadwood to save the rest of George's arm. I hadn't the heart—or even the saw—to do such a thing alone. Gently stuffing oozing flesh back into the wound, I squeezed the jagged seam together, despite his yowls of protest. Was there skin enough to stitch the wound?

I pulled a curved needle from my bag and sturdy thread, along with a bottle of aqua vitae. Lifting George's head, I poured the distilled spirits into him and prayed for the pain to ease while I threaded the needle with shaking fingers.

"Ah, balm for a sober man." Even oozing his life's blood, George managed a weak joke. "What's that yer doing?"

"Darning your socks, if I can stand the stink."

"Careful. 'S my only pair." Those were his last words for some time because I hit the back of his head with a large rock to knock him out, as I'd seen Master Whitman do before a harrowing operation. George's shocked eyes burned into my mind before his lids fluttered shut. Even unconscious, he moaned as I cleaned the wound and sewed a fine straight line, grateful that I'd learned from my mother's near-invisible stitches.

Sacahocan came to see my handiwork and dabbed her own paste of whatnot on my fine stitches. It was her apology, which I silently accepted, but who owed whom an apology in this piteous wreckage?

I knew we'd never meet again. Too much rubble lay between our two peoples. With a quick glance at Quangatarask, I helped Captain Smith carry George to the barge. We pulled up anchor, and I sank into the bottom of the boat, exhausted and sick to my core from the senseless brutality and bloodshed.

I'd bound George's wound tightly in deerskin, and he tossed beside me, shielding his eyes from the bright winter sun with his good arm.

Captain Smith steered and kicked around the baskets of corn we'd stolen at so dear a price. "Won't feed the lot of us more than a fortnight," the captain grumbled.

"We won't starve, Captain," George reminded us. His voice was husky and weak, for he'd lost much blood. "There's still those hogs fattening up on the island."

Back at the fort, Bones helped us lift George out of the boat and then hit us with the grim news: "Powhatan's slaughtered our hogs, every last one of 'em. He sent a message, said we had it comin'."

Chapter Sixteen

January, 1609, bitter cold, and Master Whitman grew worse by the hour, swinging from shivers to sweats. His eyes were veiled and rheumy. Also, the fever turned his mind topsy-turvy. "I want a fig!" he cried, then, "Bring me the leeches!" When I did, he batted the jar away, sending black worms wriggling all over our tent.

I was too exhausted to give chase but gladly cursed them. "Go back to the slimy river, you revolting bloodsuckers, you!" Easier to vent my rage on those mindless creatures than on my treacherous captain and the cruelties of warfare on both sides. I'd had enough of blood and flame to last until the next century, but now I had to deal with yet one more death.

I spooned barley gruel into Master Whitman's mouth. He clutched my shirt, pulling me down. His sour breath rocked me back.

"Elias, lad." It was the first time that he'd called me by my Christian name. "I leave ye everything I know, which is all that I have, that and a few bottles and instruments."

"Aye, sir."

"It isn't enough, now, is it?"

"Sir?"

"Ye've more in here and there"—he tapped my chest, my head—"than I can teach ye, Elias. New century, new world, and me but a craggy old man."

"Not true, Master!" True.

"Never married, never a father." He drifted off and then woke with eyes as clear as water. "Carry on for me, son, but none of that paddlewack."

"I'll use my judgment, sir, just as you've taught." Tears sprang to my eyes for the man who'd been nothing but unkind to me, nothing like my own father but who would soon be just as dead.

"Ach, Elias, ye can cure a fever and a stingray bite, but ye still can't give a decent haircut," he said and went to his Maker with a smile.

After the burial, with the Reverend Mr. Storch struggling to find generous words for Master Whitman, the tent was mine alone, but still I slept on the floor. I couldn't take the bed; it belonged to Master Whitman.

We were fewer than 50 starving souls left, praying to hang on 'til spring. Some made a porridge of our collar starch. Some chewed on shoe leather. Once I staggered out of the tent, hunger gnawing at my belly, and there stood Mistress Forrest stirring a kettle!

"Monday wash," she said. "Don't get your hopes up, son."

I found Bones and George with their heads bent toward one another, George cradling the stump of the arm Master Whitman had left him with after operating.

"No, George, we wouldn't sink that low," Bones said.

"What, you wouldn't eat fresh meat wherever you got it?"

"Not human flesh, no, sir."

Some days Captain Smith, Bones, and I were the only ones around—we as the youngest and heartiest—and the captain because of his hidden supply of food.

He took some men ice fishing. The promise of fish and oysters roused us all to dance around the fire again. How different the natives' dances were from our own—and us without a drum to our name.

"Sing the ditty that the Indian girl sang you," George said.

I sang what I remembered and made up the rest; how would they know?

All was quiet between the Indians and us. I suppose their appetite for warfare dwindled along with the embers of their villages and the last of the winter's food.

Then one day in March Sacahocan and

Quangatarask walked into the fort, covered with deerskin but still barefoot. We'd not been face-to-face since the terrible fire in her village.

"Hallo!" I called, selfishly hoping they'd brought a bit of dried meat or shriveled corn. Quangatarask ran to me. I smoothed the ragged burn scar on his arm, pink as pigskin.

Sacahocan had taught him a new word: "Horse-horse-horse!"

I hoisted him onto my bony hip and carried him to the stable. He hung on the door and chatted with Machiavelli, the only one of our horses that hadn't found his way into our stew pot, since he belonged to Captain Smith.

So much I wanted to tell Sacahocan but first, "I'm ashamed and sorry for what my countrymen did to your village."

She shrugged, and I was sad to see how resigned she was to the terrible brutality of our two peoples. I would *never* get used to it. She said, "I know you came to my village to heal, not to burn, Ly-iss."

Behind us Quangatarask whinnied in chorus with Machiavelli, who was glad for the company. I caught sight of Bones peeking from behind the stable. He'd been teasing me about being sweet on the Indian girl. Hah!

She said, "I come to say good-bye."

My heart plummeted. "Where are you going?"

"When the land is tired, we move to greener fields—but not yet. Most girls my age go to a husband."

"So young?" I was years, decades, off from marriage! Maybe never. The doctor's lot was not suited to family life.

"Not young for Pamunkee. But for me, it will be hard to find a good man who would marry with a medicine woman. Not easy to live with me, for I see things others do not want to know."

"What do you see in me, Sacahocan?"

She studied me closely, those intense gray eyes baring my soul. Again she reminded me of my sister Catherine, and suddenly the thought struck me: she'd had an English father! But I was too embarrassed to ask for sure.

Sacahocan said, "You will go back to your native land."

Yes, that's what I wanted, my city and family. But as soon as the thought escaped me, I knew it was no longer true. "This is my home now, Sacahocan."

And what did that tell her? That I was no different from my countrymen, claiming her people's land for myself?

"In the season of falling leaves, Ly-iss, your father, your chief, will suffer a terrible burn, and you will sail home with him to learn in your own land. One day you will come back to my rivers and forests, a great medicine man."

I beamed at her glorious prophecy for me and for our people—that Indian and English could share this beautiful land. "And you, Sacahocan?"

Her strange eyes sparkled. "Tomorrow Quangatarask and I go to Werowocomoco. I will learn at the feet of the master Dream-Reader how to heal my people deep within. Your people do not have Dream-Readers, do you?"

Of course we did, but the Bible would be too hard to explain to her.

Her hands were tucked under her deerskin mantle. She danced up and down to warm her feet. "Someday I will be the mother of many daughters, and when I am wrinkled with age, maybe I will be chief of the Pamunkee."

"Chief! Women can do that?"

"Horse-horse-horse!" Quangatarask sang behind me. I glanced at him, just as Bones ducked out of sight. Rascal!

Behind the stable stood a tree. Yesterday it had been nothing but brittle winter sticks, but now pale green dots promised buds for the summer shade that would make Machiavelli's lonely life more tolerable.

Truly, my new home, this Virginia, was an amazing land. Native girls could be chiefs, and poor London boys could be doctors.

And peace between the Indians and the English? Anything was possible—even spring.

Now flip over and read
Sacahocan's side of the story!

Journey to Jamestown

SACAHOCAN'S STORY

KINGFISHER
a Houghton Mifflin Company imprint
222 Berkeley Street
Boston, Massachusetts 02116
www.houghtonmifflinbooks.com

First published in 2005
2 4 6 8 10 9 7 5 3 1

LIBRARY OF CONGRESS CATALOGING-IN-PUBLICATION DATA
has been applied for.

ISBN 0-7534-5796-2
ISBN 978-07534-5796-2

Printed in India
1TR/0105/THOM/SGCH/90NS

MY SIDE OF THE STORY

Journey to Jamestown

SACAHOCAN'S STORY

LOIS RUBY

BOSTON

Have you read Elias's side of the story?
If you haven't, flip back and read it first;
if you have, you can now read
Sacahocan's side of the story!

Chapter One

Little Brother's face is like the moon. It is round and sometimes glows, but often a dark shadow slides across it. He almost never sleeps. That is why our mother named him Quangatarask, "owl," for his eyes are wide at night, watching everything, as if he guards us while we sleep.

Our mother says, "Sacahocan, this stew I turn and stir, daughter, see? Squash and corn and deer flesh swimming together?"

I gaze into the clay pot simmering over the fire and breathe in the rich aroma. Mother lifts a spoonful to my mouth. Delicious!

"That's what it's like inside Quangatarask's head," she says, "everything mixed up, but the result is pleasing." She pats Little Brother's head. His dark owl eyes stare up at her. He does not understand things like other boys do. Beginning when he was three summers old, our mother took him into the woods each morning before breakfast to teach him the ways of a bow that she'd made from strips of the locust tree and a string of deer hide. She showed him how to plant his feet on the loamy ground, how to flex his arms and shoulders to pull back the bow and release the arrow. Hopeless. Yet Mother patiently takes him out morning after morning. I could shoot a squirrel out of a tree when I was four summers. Now nine more summers have passed, and what use is it for a girl to shoot straight?

"You have other gifts," Mother reminds me. I am learning the ways of healing, but I cannot mend my brother. In a few summers he will be ready for *huskanaw*, the ceremony where the boys run between rows of elder warriors who beat them with sticks. How can he understand that this is the way boys are shaped into men? How can he live alone in the forest for nights and weeks, with nothing to eat and little to drink? When the visions come, they will terrify him. If he survives, what will happen when he cannot pull a bow and sight deer or bear? They will see him first! He will not be able to go on the hunt with the other men or defend himself in battle.

Quangatarask's father, who is not my father, says, "Pah, there will be nothing left for my son but women's work." What is wrong with women's work? We are medicine women and sometimes lead our clans and tribes. We plant and harvest, gather nuts and berries and herbs, carry home wood and thatch for the houses we build with our own hands. We mend and weave and sew. But such things are not fitting for a young man.

Mother says, "Keep your tongue, husband. The boy will find his way."

"Find his way into a bear's den," his father says.

I do not like Quangatarask's father. My own father was not one of us. He was a foreigner who came here many years ago. He lived for two seasons on Roanoke Island, miles from our home. When his people were driven away by hunger and scattered into many corners, my father wandered into our camp clothed in tatters of strange fabric and ranting like the Spirits had overtaken him. Our men would have shot him through with arrows if my mother hadn't come running out of her parents' *yihakan* at that moment with a basket of clothes to be washed in the river. She tripped over a tree root, and the clothes flew and landed at the feet of the stranger with the yellow hair and beard that straggled halfway down his chest. Though there were arrows aimed at him from all four directions, he bent to pick up the clothes and placed them back in my mother's basket. Her elder brother saw the love in her eyes and called off the kill.

My father, who wasn't my father yet, had been walking for days, maybe weeks, and was half starved. They say he ate from the time the sun was highest in the sky until it set, chewing and lapping without pause.

So we Pamunkee took him in, he married my mother, and I am their child. I am called Strange Eyes because my eyes are as gray as the river in the winter and as green as grape leaves in the spring. My people say such eyes are frightening, that they see back in time, and they see forward.

I only see what I see.

Strange Eyes is not my real name. When I was eight summers, just before my father died of the last wave of fever that rampaged through our village, my mother began to call me Sacahocan, which means "picture writing." My father had been teaching me to make his foreign words with sticks in the dirt or with charcoal on deer hide. I could already speak his language, but now I could also write it, and our people thought this was as amazing as the sprouting of new fruit each spring. Imagine, I could draw tiny pictures that my father could read back to me just as I wrote them, word by word! None of us Pamunkee, in fact, no one in the entire Powhatan Empire, could do such a thing, except maybe the great Chief Powhatan himself.

I do not look like other girls in my village. My hair is not black and thick and straight like the tail of a deer. Everyone knows that a child is the combined image of her mother and father, so my hair is brown as hemp, thin and fine and a little wavy. I am the only one in my village fathered by a foreigner. Also, my people are ashamed of Quangatarask, who will never be a warrior.

Most of the day Little Brother is at my side. In the spring I plant the seeds, and I tend the shoots in the summer. I hand him a basket of small stones, and each day he looks at them as though he's never seen rocks before.

"Remember, Quangatarask, you have an important job. Stay there and watch for raccoons," I tell him time and again, but he keeps running out of the scarecrow house to follow every squirrel on the ground—he would fly to each passing bird if he could sprout wings. Little Brother is very good at gently scaring away small insects to save my plants, but he cannot throw rocks at raccoons all of his life, can he?

And I cannot always be at his side, for I am told I have *manito*, the sacred medicine power, passed down from my mother, and I must go to the *powa* rocks to welcome the Spirits and prepare for my dream vision during the *hobbomak*. I stood proud and straight beside Rassoum, our medicine man, when Chief Opechancanough chose me for this ceremony, but in my secret heart I was frightened. Some have returned with their words wild and ranting so that no one can understand them for weeks.

From Mother and Rassoum, I am learning how the press of hands on an ailing body can tell you where the hurt is and how the herbs that grow around our village can tell you what their use is. But from my father, I learned the importance of words, spoken and written. To think that I might return from the *hobbomak* unable to talk to my people scares me more than anything I can imagine—except Quangatarask in a bear's jaws.

Chapter Two

Just when our hopes soar that they will go back to where they came from, more English arrive on a boat so big that ten of our canoes laid side by side wouldn't touch the walls. Kecuttannowas brings us the news. Chief Opechancanough, one of our three *weroances*, sends him to spy on the foreigners, but he has not been able to learn how many seasons they plan to stay along our river, which they call the James river after their great chief in far-off England.

"Two years is too long," Kecuttannowas says.

"Two seasons," his brother says.

"Two days," says the next brother.

"Two minutes . . . "

Kecuttannowas has more brothers than sense.

Quangatarask pulls on my dress. "We go see the foreigners!"

Little Brother and I walk for miles and hide behind the yellow pines to watch them. "You must be very quiet, Quangatarask."

He can't help himself: "Look at them!"

"Shh!"

"Funny-funny."

"Quiet, please."

"But the sun beats down. Why do they wear clothes and moccasins up to their knees?"

"Quiet!" Little Brother does not understand that these foreigners fire at our people with their thundering weapons that spit stones right through a person's chest and leave a bleeding hole as large as a plum. We should run the other way. Yet, I am curious, like Quangatarask, because these are my father's people, and I am like them, a little.

We watch them making buildings with logs they have stolen from our forests. Our houses cover us well, but they are simple and light so that we can move to greener fields when we have drawn out whatever Mother Earth has to give us. These houses, the English ones, are much sturdier, as if they mean to stay in our territory more than a season or two. A high fence surrounds their village, with guards posted, looking for—what? We mean them no harm, and their guns would do worse to us than our warriors could do to them.

I see only men, young and old. Where are the women? Do the men make them stay inside the houses? How terrible. Our women build and farm and fish and take the laundry to the stream and roam freely through our villages. Quangatarask tugs on my mantle, pointing to dogs lying in the shade or lapping at buckets of water. The dogs have more freedom than English women!

I am lucky to live among the Pamunkee people, even if there I am called Strange Eyes.

"Come, Little Brother, we must go home before Mother worries."

"No!" Quangatarask digs his heels into the soft earth. I have to drag him until his knees lock. As quickly as he protested, he has forgotten, so I march him in front of me, his little flat feet plodding along and kicking dust in my face.

Footsteps behind us! Foreigners! I pull Quangatarask to the ground, and soon someone passes without noticing us behind the loblolly tree. Ah, not a foreigner, but I cannot tell from behind if he is Pamunkee or one of our enemies who would gladly capture a woman and child to increase their own wealth. I clap my hand on Quangatarask's mouth, but I might as well be trying to silence a seagull.

"Hall-o!" he cries out and breaks away from me. The painted warrior spins around. It is Kecuttannowas, one of us!

"Sacahocan, what are you doing here?" His words are angry, but his face looks pleased to see me.

"We've been watching the English."

"Very dangerous," he warns, and he knows this well. He is Chief Opechancanough's main spy. Kecuttannowas has lived 15 summers and is a skillful lone hunter. I have watched him stalk game. He would fool the cleverest buck in the forest, wearing deerskin over his arm and a doe's head stuffed with moss and straw on a stick. He taunts his prey, darting from one tree to another until he is near enough to send an arrow whirring into the deer's flank. He is as quick as lightning. Kecuttannowas's name means lightning, and sometimes his anger streaks across our village like a bolt of the very thing he's named after.

He is already starting to bend poles of green wood into the arch of a house, and his mother is weaving mats. He brings Mother lavish gifts of fresh venison and widemouthed bass. This only means one thing. Good heavens! He has said more than once, "I will marry you, Sacahocan." I laugh and turn away, but he does not give up. He is pleasing to look at—tall and lean as a young willow, and the colorful wolf markings on his arms are artfully done. He has a dip in his chin deep enough to hold the pit of a cherry, as if his mother poked a finger in the dough that became Kecuttannowas! He is on his way to being a rich man, a good marriage prospect, but I am not planning to marry anyone—and certainly not him.

Kecuttannowas, Lightning, does not like Little Brother, but he sweeps him into his arms and carries him on his back because Quangatarask is a doorway to my heart.

"What did you hear?" I ask.

"The foreigners are building their fort again. I thought when it burned down in the winter that would be the end of them. Now there are one hundred more." He glances at me with a funny smile. "But no women."

"I noticed. And no children?"

"I've seen two. One is new, a boy of twelve or thirteen summers. They say he comes with their medicine man. He'll be busy. There are sick and dying everywhere."

"Lightning, isn't it odd that the English have no fields of corn and no nets and weirs in the water? I see no one in the forest hunting deer or otters or rabbits. What on earth do they eat?"

"Each other," Lightning says.

Chapter Three

"Kick the ball, Quangatarask!" I shout. "Kick it!" The boys run like young deer, moving the ball up and down the field, but Little Brother is rooted like a tree, and the ball hits him in the head. Again. Oh! I whistle for him to come to me.

The boys are laughing and panting because the game tires even brave hunters. One boy, Tall Tree, is not very tall yet, but his mother has great hopes for him. He doubles over, hands on his knees, to catch his breath. Then he folds to the ground, thrashing around like a fish on a hook.

"Stay here, Quangatarask." I rush onto the field and listen to Tall Tree's chest. His breath whistles as though he's pushing it through pebbles.

"Carry him to my mother's house," I instruct the players, "and send for Rassoum."

Rassoum is our medicine man and my teacher. I hurry along with the bearers as Tall Tree's body sags between them. Calmly, I say, "Tall Tree, try to let your muscles go. Take shallow breaths. That's the way, good," but he is still gasping for what life breath he can suck from the air.

The shelf above my bed is cluttered with bottles, which I knock over looking for the right one. The black one, yes, there it is. Mother hands me a cup of boiling water. The medicinal leaves float on the water, swell, sink, and rise to the top again. "Hurry!" I order them, but I know the leaves will have to steep many minutes for the remedy to work. Tall Tree is coughing, which is good, but between coughs he clutches the air for clear breath. Mother bathes his face and neck with cool water, deeply breathing as if her breath might go into him.

Rassoum comes and chants to the Spirits, shaking a gourd rattle in one hand and beating his own chest with the other. I tell him what I have done so far. He nods, circling and shaking the rattle over Tall Tree. The rattle clatters to the ground when Rassoum presses his palms on Tall Tree's heaving chest. He wheezes as though breathing through a thin reed.

Rassoum checks the leaves, nodding that the concoction is ready, and we pour it into Tall Tree as quickly as he can swallow. Minutes pass. Rassoum chants. Then Tall Tree's chest begins to relax, no longer puffing out like a bladder of water. Color returns to his face, he stops kicking and starts breathing normally.

Rassoum and I offer a prayer of thanks to the Spirit within the plant that gives us relief and to the Spirit within our hands that allows us to heal. When

Tall Tree is strong and able to walk to his own house, I plume with pride, a soaring eagle!

My wings are quickly clipped. Rassoum tells me what I did that I should not have done and what I should have done that I did not do. Behind him, my mother nods in agreement.

I have much to learn.

We go to the *quiocosin*, the priest's house that sits high up above our village. It is large enough to hold the bodies of all our *weroances* and *weroansquas*—those men and women who have been our rulers since earliest memory—that rest there eternally.

The priest looks up from the fire he tends at the eastern door. His ample body blocks all the light into the house. "Sacahocan and venerable Rassoum, what brings you to me this day?"

Rassoum pokes me with his elbow.

I try to sound humble: "We have saved a boy from a journey to the rising sun. We come to offer thanks."

The priest dips his head, encouraging us to do the proper thing. We set shell beads and blue corn kernels at the feet of the Spirits' statues and scatter cured tobacco leaves over the fire. The priest claps his hands soundlessly, approving and then dismissing us. His loose jowls shake as he bends to tend the fire again. It is probably evil of me to say this—and Okeus, spirit of all human striving, please do not strike me dumb—but the truth is that the priests grow very fat because we shower them with our best foods, and they never get exercise. How laughable to imagine a priest running up and down the field with the young hunters!

"What brings laughter to your eyes, Sacahocan?" asks Rassoum.

I straighten up. "Nothing. Just the pleasure of seeing Tall Tree strong again."

Rassoum sends me a playful smile. He knows me better than my own mother does. Suddenly I remember Little Brother. Poor child, he is probably still standing at the side of the field, waiting for me.

Long shadows lie across the deserted field. When I tell Quangatarask in a certain voice to stay, it is as though I've sewn his feet to the very spot. He never wanders away.

But now he seems to have vanished like billowing smoke into the heavens.

I rush past Quangatarask's father into our house. "Mother, is Little Brother here?"

She is sewing a hole in our window skin. "No, daughter. I haven't seen the little scamp since our noon meal. I thought he was with you."

"He is. Was." I dash past Quangatarask's frowning

father again. I peek in all of the nearby houses, but no one has seen him. I race back again, leaping over the father's stretched-out feet to answer Mother's question with a shrug of my shoulders.

"Where is that child?" she murmurs, her face twisted with worry. "We must find him before his father asks for him." I think she is a little bit afraid of Quangatarask's father, as I am. "Please, daughter, find the boy, go."

I search in the places I have taken my brother in the past weeks. He might be hiding among the cattails or wading out to catch clams or dreaming under a sweet gum tree, with the fallen leaves a bed of red and gold beneath him. But he is in none of those places. I ask everyone along the way: "Have you seen Quangatarask? Have you?"

No one has seen him, and now everyone begins looking, though some, I know, will be happy if he never shows his face in Menapacute again.

Chapter Four

I weave white feathers into my hair and bring food to the *quiocosin*, the temple, to place at the foot of the god Okeus.

"Back so soon, Sacahocan?" says the priest.

"It's my brother, Quangatarask. He's disappeared. I must ask the Spirits to tell me which way to go to find him."

I'm sorry I thought the priests were fat, I tell myself, sprinkling more tobacco leaves onto the fire to honor the Spirits. Waiting, waiting for their guidance.

Then a voice speaks inside my head: *The child is in the village of the foreigners.*

No! I run out to the big *yihakan* where Chief Opechancanough lives and call to his watchers at the door. "My brother has wandered into the camp of the foreigners!" Quickly, the door flaps shut.

The chief's thunderous voice roars: "We will not let the barbarians steal one of our children. Lightning knows the intruders' camp best. Dispatch him at once, with two warriors. Go."

They come flying out of the house, knocking me into the dirt and bolting through the village to gather men, water, bows, and knives to bring my brother back.

When our hunters reach the English village, which will fire first—Lightning's arrow or the foreigner's fire stick? Will Little Brother be caught in their shooting? I would die if I lost him!

I do not plan to follow, but if your feet move, you cannot stay back weaving baskets, and my feet are leading me to the foreigners' camp, two or three trees behind the hunters.

They do not know that a girl hears every word they speak over a trip of many hours. The worst is this. Cougar says, "We should leave the boy with the barbarians. He wouldn't live through *huskanaw* anyway. You barely survived it yourself, Deer Knife."

Deer Knife ignores Cougar's rude comment. "His sister won't let harm come to him."

Cougar says, "She can't keep her Strange Eyes on him every minute. Better to let the boy die at the hands of the barbarians than to be eaten alive by a brown bear."

Lightning's voice is grim and determined: "Chief Opechancanough sends us to rescue the boy, and that is what we will do."

"Pah!" says Cougar. "If he weren't your sweetheart's brother, you'd agree with me, say it."

Breathlessly, I wait for Lightning's answer, long in coming.

"True."

Fury rises in my throat, and I want to shout at him, but what good would this do for Quangatarask? Besides, we are drawing close to the English village now. I follow a squirrel up an oak tree to watch.

Lightning and Deer Knife and Cougar approach the village with bows drawn. Six foreigners stand guard at the top of the palisade, guns aimed at the hunters.

"Move a muscle, red man, and I'll blow yer brains out."

The hunters freeze like deer, wait, and then Cougar takes a step forward. Gunfire rips through the air, and Cougar sinks into a pile of brittle leaves at Deer Knife's feet. Lightning kneels to check for breathing. He'll be shot! But the English do not notice or they think one dead Pamunkee is enough for a day's work. Lightning slings Cougar's limp body over his back, motions to Deer Knife, and they retreat through the thick forest. Should I follow? Tears spring to my eyes. I will not cry, will not. Cougar has died honorably, even if the white killer had no reason to shoot a young hunter who had come in peace. Shame flames my cheeks to think that I was spawned by such a people, and now the barbarians have Quangatarask!

From my perch high in the oak tree I see into the

clearing. Little Brother stands in the arms of the medicine man's boy, surrounded by foreigners. I scuttle down the tree. One careful step after another, I make my way into the camp. They watch my every step. I will snatch Quangatarask away, march him right back to our village, and be done with the foreigners forever.

The medicine man's boy is no killer. I see in his eyes the sorrow and shame for Cougar's senseless death, though he never says a word about it. So we talk haltingly. His language does not come easily to my lips after so long. His name is Ly-iss. His eyes swim with kindness; he would not hurt Little Brother or any of us. His father stands nearby, with hair like the boy's, the color of fallen leaves, and even more of it on his chin. Lightning had told me that the fall-leaf man is the *weroance* of the village. So small a chief? Our chiefs are like strong poles. We must bend our heads back to see their faces.

Quangatarask attaches himself to Ly-iss. I have to pry him away, expecting the slurping sounds of an oyster coming loose from its shell.

Many eyes are on me as I lead Little Brother away. These foreigners have been known to shoot us in the back, but even they would not shoot women and children, would they? I push Little Brother ahead of me and start walking, then running when we are safely away from them. The more ground we cover, the better, before Quangatarask gets so tired that I have to carry him on my shoulders through the dark forest.

Home in our village, young people gather around to hear the story while their fathers build the burial platform and swear revenge and their mothers blacken their faces with coal and pour their grief into preparing mats to wrap Cougar's shattered body in.

My friends have a thousand questions:

"What was it like in the foreigners' camp?"

"Do they smell like rotten meat?"

"Do they hide nuts and berries in all that fur on their faces?"

"Do they have hair on their chests?"

"Where are their women? We've heard that the men birth their babies—is it true?"

"Sacahocan, were you scared of the barbarians?"

"Only a little," I reply bravely, but the roar of guns firing storms through my head. Still, how can you be afraid of so many men whose stomachs are growling with hunger? I promise myself that after we bury Cougar I will bring the foreigners corn, as much as I can carry, and wild strawberries and sassafras and snakeroot herbs for the medicine man's boy, to thank him. It was not Ly-iss who shot the gun that tore through Cougar's body.

But I must hurry to the foreigners' village and back, for Chief Opechancanough will surely send warriors into the camp. It is a simple rule of warfare that every civilized person must know: you cannot kill one of ours without sacrificing one of yours.

That chance comes the night we bury Cougar. Lightning proudly tells the story as our whole village sits around the night fire, men on one side, women on the other. I strain to hear every word across the circle.

"The village slept when I crept into their camp. My heart's wish was to shoot their chief. I know where he sleeps. But some drunken fool stumbled out of his tent and saw my eyes gleaming in the moonlight. He opened his hairy mouth to roar for help. I shot before a sound came out."

"Dead?" Deer Knife asks.

"Dead? Pah! The arrowhead jammed right into his beating heart. He fell back, and I shoved the arrow into his chest until the feathers were buried in his flesh."

"Well done!" the other hunters shout, slapping one another on their backs. Cougar's mother weeps quietly beside my mother, and I remember something my father had said from his holy book: an eye for an eye.

We are even now.

Chapter Five

During the corn harvest season we rejoice in the plenty that Mother Earth gives us. Brightly painted and feathered, we sing and dance into the night. Quangatarask loves to dance. Those corn-gathering nights are so joyous that even his father dances, lifting Little Brother to his shoulders. Our mother says, "Quangatarask has ears for drumming that the rest of us are too busy to hear." I watch his little legs kicking his father's chest according to his own beat.

Everyone dances, the young and the grandfathers and grandmothers, but Lightning does not join us. I find him sitting alone behind the circle of houses, carving a wolf's face by the generous light of the moon.

"Why are you not dancing, Lightning?"

He pretends not to hear, whittling away splinters of black walnut.

"Are you mourning for Cougar?" We all mourned as Cougar's body was covered with earth. We'd danced then, too, as is the way of our people, because we knew that Cougar had gone to the land of the Spirits and also that in the fullness of time his bones would be dug up to join his family's bones forever.

"Men die in battle every day," Lightning says, shrugging his broad, painted shoulders.

"And you bravely avenged his death. So, what, then?"

"This: Chief Opechancanough sent me to bring your brother back, and I failed."

"Oh, Lightning, no! If you had gone one step into the foreigners' camp, you wouldn't be alive now to carve that fine wolf's head."

He throws his knife at a tree, where it vibrates and sticks. "You were brave enough to do what I could not do. You, a girl."

Yes, but I had foolishly walked right into the camp without thinking. "I don't know why they chose to let me enter the camp. My bones could be moldering like Cougar's now."

"You are alive," Lightning mutters, as though he regrets the fact that I still draw breath, and that makes me angry.

Strange how I slide from friendship to anger and back a hundred times in the course of a conversation with Lightning. "You wish both of us were dead! Myself and Quangatarask!"

Lightning gets up to yank his knife out of the tree. "Not you," he says. He spins around, waving the knife. "Think, Sacahocan. Quangatarask has a sister called Strange Eyes because she's the daughter of a foreigner. He has a lazy, worthless father, he has a mother who dreams the impossible for him, but we all know he'll be a child even when he's old enough to be a father. What future does he have? No work, no purpose, no brain."

I have the advantage of a surprise attack. I grab the knife out of Lightning's hand and hold it to his throat. "Never, ever say such a thing about my brother, do you hear me?"

"How could I not hear you when you're shouting in my ear?"

I nick his skin with the tip of the knife. "Do you hear me more clearly now?"

He easily grabs the knife and slides it into the pouch on his waist. "When we marry, I'll be sure to keep knives out of your reach."

"I will never marry you, Kecuttannowas."

"We will see," he says, and he pulls the knife out and begins carving again.

"Where is Ly-iss?" Quangatarask asks.

I am sweeping the dust and grit outside our house. "Far away, with the foreigners, and don't be thinking of walking there again, Little Brother."

"I want to see Ly-iss!" He stamps his feet, scattering the sweepings I'd just gathered. "Ly-iss, Ly-iss!" he cries until he sounds like a hissing snake.

I sigh. "Tomorrow, if there is no rain." I scan the skies, hoping for clouds. "Let's go watch the men make canoes, Little Brother."

"Watch canoes!" He grabs the broom out of my hand, and we run to the clearing near the river.

A hollowed-out log, cut from our forest, lies lengthwise across wooden poles. A small fire burns in its center to loosen the wood. Deer Knife chips out the burned flesh of the tree with sharp shells, smoothing it until it shines like his own skin.

"How many will paddle this canoe when it's finished?" I ask.

Deer Knife answers, "Only two or three." Scritch-scritch. The scraping of shell against wood makes my teeth ache. "It'll be small enough to get through the marshes if you and your mother go hunting for reeds to weave or to fish in the Pamunkee river or for two warriors to sneak up on the Susquehannocks up north. It would be a pleasure to battle someone besides the foreigners."

At the mention of the word Quangatarask starts hissing again: "Ly-iss! Ly-iss!"

"The English boy," I explain. A curious look crosses Deer Knife's face, and I quickly remind him, "Ly-iss is not the one who shot Cougar, you know. He's the medicine man's boy, learning like I am."

Deer Knife jumps into the boat to control the small fire. "I don't trust any of the whiteskins," he sputters. "What do they want with us?"

I look all around at the tall pines, the blue heavens, the land that stretches as far as I can see, to the ocean that I know lies beyond. "Is there not room enough for the English and us, Deer Knife?"

"Not if they mean to take the land where our crops grow and the forests where our animals live and drive us into the sea."

Quangatarask's owl eyes are fixed on Deer Knife, though I'm sure he has not understood any words that Deer Knife spoke.

"Come, little man." Deer Knife pulls Quangatarask into the canoe. "When our work is done here, you and I will paddle this canoe into the marshes, and we'll spear fish for our dinner."

"Fish!" Little Brother cries, waving his palm like a shad wriggling through river water.

My heart leaps at Deer Knife's kindness. If only the best strands of Lightning and the best threads of Deer Knife were woven into one fine cloth, then Quangatarask and I would both be warmly covered.

Chapter Six

"Shh!" Rassoum hushes me as I hurry into his house. He kneels before the mat of Graywolf, one of our elders, whose face is the color of a rainstorm. His sunken eyes are like rocks in wet sand and are circled in black. His body shivers with fever, yet sweat pours down his cheeks. Rassoum pries Graywolf's mouth open to show me a swollen tongue so white that it looks like he has been drinking doe's milk.

Rassoum works a plug of tobacco in his cheek to soften it for Graywolf. He blows on Graywolf's face and chest to chase the illness away. Graywolf flinches at the mist of cool breath on his feverish body.

Rassoum motions for me to come closer and thrusts a long feather into my hand. I pass the feather over the length of Graywolf, never touching him, to find places where Graywolf's body throbs with mysterious energies. This is how we learn where illness dwells deep in a person's body.

The feather begins to flutter as Graywolf's breathing quickens. Yes, there in Graywolf's chest I find it, but it feels different from any other illness I've learned. Still, I brush it into a pile for Rassoum to do the rest. He removes the softened tobacco from his mouth and tucks it into Graywolf's cheek. Tobacco can work magic.

Rassoum turns away from Graywolf and me. He is putting bits of bone and shell in his mouth as spirit helpers. He turns back, knife raised, and quickly makes three slashes in the air a knuckle's distance above Graywolf's chest.

"Aye!" Graywolf cries, for he feels the cuts as if they have actually sliced his flesh.

Rassoum bends to Graywolf's chest as though he was sucking the marrow of a juicy bone. He pulls the disease out and holds it in his mouth so it will not reenter Graywolf's weakened body. Rassoum nods for me to chant the words for this ritual, a song to the Spirits. After the fourth verse he spits out the spirit helpers, those splinters of shell and bone, into a jar, along with the disease. I hurry outside to bury the jar far from our circle of houses, relieved that the illness is gone and cannot return to our people. Before the rising of the sun Graywolf will be well!

By sunrise, Graywolf is dead.

Others come to us with illnesses like his. Rassoum's worried eyes remind me that this is how my father and many others among us in that season died. Now we give them the black drink made from a brew of holly shrubs. We boil roots of milkweed until they are soft and place these on the heads and chests of our patients. We give them snakeroot to chew. They die anyway. More come. Rassoum carries them into the steam house and prays that the heat will draw the illness out and send it billowing to the heavens, away from us. We thank the Spirits and beg the Spirits, and still our patients die.

"What else can we do, Rassoum?" I cry, exhausted from tending the sick on so many nights and their burials on so many days. I have never seen my teacher so discouraged, nor so ragged with sleeplessness and worry. When he isn't caring for our patients, he is chanting, chanting, until his voice is thin and he croaks like a frog. Finally, the Spirits speak to him.

"We must call for a Dream-Reader," Rassoum says, barely above a whisper. "Go, Sacahocan, and ask Opechancanough to send a messenger to Chief Powhatan. He must bring back the best Dream-Reader in all of Tsenacommacah." He points his shaking finger toward the door. Poor weary man, he leans against the mat covering the wall, chanting even as he sleeps. I run like the wind, wondering if the English medicine man's boy has a cure. But I cannot go to the foreigners' village now. Here is where I am needed.

Rassoum has been teaching me to pay attention and learn from everything Mother Nature offers. Now, desperate, I run to listen to the flowers, the trees shedding their leaves. I study how the clouds move across the sky, how the water ripples in the streams. I watch otters at play, chipmunks burrowing into holes in the trees, bucks and does listening for sounds in the forest. Each plant, each animal, each stone, each star contains a spirit that I could communicate with—if only I knew how. Rassoum promised me that in another cycle of seasons, possibly two, their quiet messages will come through to me. "Practice, faith, patience," he sings again and again. But my impatience gnaws away at me like a wolf with a bone, and the Spirits only murmur; I cannot read their messages yet.

And then my mother lies on a mat in Rassoum's house, shivering and tossing with fever like Graywolf, like my father, and I am terrified that Quangatarask and I will lose her. Strange red bumps erupt on her skin that drive her crazy with itching. I bathe her burnished skin, wave the smoke of burning twigs of sweetgrass and sage her way, but she continues to toss on her mat.

Her husband comes with Quangatarask on his hip, bearing chips of cedar to burn. His eyes cry, and this is how I know that he loves her, although he rarely shows it. He leaves Little Brother with us. "He will give her strength," he says and quickly ducks out the door. Quangatarask stands at my side, eyes wide, whimpering.

Lightning brings corn cakes and wild turkey stew from his mother's house and no words for me. Hours pass. Quangatarask dozes beside Mother and wakes with fear blazing in his eyes. He knows that we are losing her.

Deer Knife comes and carries Quangatarask away, saying only, "My canoe is finished, and I've made a paddle just for you, little man." My eyes thank him while Mother thrashes around and raves nonsense words coined by the burning fever. I look to Rassoum—surely he will do something for her! He only shakes his head. And then there is nothing left but to wait for the Dream-Reader.

Chapter Seven

Everyone is busy harvesting corn when the Dream-Reader comes, his white mantle billowing and our hunter trailing him. The Dream-Reader's name is Apowa, meaning Dream-Energy. He is very old, perhaps 80 summers. His frail bones would scatter to the wind without his shriveled hide sheltering them.

Mother sleeps fitfully in Rassoum's house, with the smoke of the fire hazy around her.

"Her name?" he asks.

I barely trust my voice, so close to tears. "Sandpiper, Dream-Reader."

"Ah, a small bird. That helps me understand where she flies to. When we sleep," he explains in his wavery voice, "our spirits travel throughout the earth and sky. Your mother will awaken, and she will tell me of her travels. Then we will know how to cure her." He gently prods Mother awake. "Where have you traveled to, Sister Sandpiper?"

Her tight face relaxes now that she is in the hands of the Dream-Reader. She begins to whisper her dreams—torn fragments of cloth pulled through her feverish sleep. The Dream-Reader puts his ear to Mother's mouth to catch every word. Rassoum and I watch closely. Rassoum is too old, but I may still learn to be a Dream-Reader.

Mother's lips stop moving, her eyes close. Her spirit has left her forever! I clutch Quangatarask, who is still like a tree stump, owl eyes unblinking.

The Dream-Reader stands up. "Here is what you will do, Sacahocan." So, she still lives! I listen with wet eyes and a grateful heart.

Quangatarask lies down beside her. Her trembling arm reaches out to pull him near. How I wish I was six summers again, to lie there beside my mother and force her well with my own health and energy. But I must follow the Dream-Reader's instructions—every chant, every gesture, every herb, every touch.

Of all our patients with this strange new illness, Mother alone survives!

I carry Quangatarask to the river, and we dive in to thank the *manito aki* of the water. But when I return to Rassoum's house, I find three more people burning with fever, and the Dream-Reader is gone. Rassoum and I work through the night.

We lose them all, every man, woman, and child.

Late at night I watch the movement of the moon and stars across the sky. I sleep under the stars, away from the noise of our village, to listen and hear what they have to tell me. We can do little to save our people from this illness, from the death of the body and release of the spirit to the sun. Mother's cure is a miracle, but it is not the answer. There is no answer. Unless the foreigners' medicine has its own magic.

When I awake the next morning, all becomes clear to me. How foolish to think the English would provide magic for us! No, the Great Spirits are angry with us, and that is why so many of our people fall prey to the strange new sickness. Everything in our lives is connected in a magical circle. What jabs one point in the circle pushes every other point out of place. But what have we Pamunkee done to cause the Spirits to be so displeased? I must find out. Only then can I learn how to bring our lives back in harmony with the rest of Mother Nature's creatures.

I do not eat. I take only small sips of water to keep the parts of my mouth from sticking together. After three days I am an empty vessel, like Deer Knife's canoe, hollowed out, scraped smooth.

"You're too thin," Mother says, setting a bowl of oyster soup on the ground between us.

I edge away from the bowl. "You used to tell me I ate too much and that I'd grow so fat that no one would want to marry me."

"No one will marry you if you're as skinny as a

corn stalk." Mother moves the bowl closer, stirring it to release a tantalizing smell.

"Maybe I will never marry. Maybe that is what the Great Spirits have in mind for me."

Her spoon clatters against the bowl in shock. "Never marry? What makes you think that would please the Spirits? We're meant to be born, grow, take mates, give birth, die, and go on to the next world. The babies we bring into this world then begin the cycle all over again. They are our immortality."

I sigh deeply, trying to ignore the cries of my body for water. I have stopped feeling hungry—but the thirst? Oh! Even awake I dream of buckets of water raining over me, my mouth open wide to swallow great gulps of it and the rest soaking my skin that is as dry as deer hide.

"If you don't marry, daughter, the line of my ancestors ends with you," Mother says sadly. She lifts the bowl to my hands. The warmth ripples up my arm, and the aroma reawakens my hunger. Oh, I am tempted, so tempted, but I close my eyes and pray for the hour when I will not be clouded by the need for food and water. Then will my mind be open to hear the teachings of the Spirits.

"All right, daughter," Mother says, resigned to my stubbornness. "I'll take you to the healing place." She staggers to her feet, still weak from her illness. She reaches for my hand to pull me up. Longingly, I leave the bowl of oyster soup on the ground and follow Mother to the women's steam house.

This will be my first time, and I wonder will I be strong enough to endure the heat and steam that pulls the energy right out of a body? Can I be silent for so many minutes, when words flood me all the time? Most worrisome, will I be able to leave my body and fly to the place the Spirits call me to? And will I know how to get back, or will I forever float between this firm earth and the mist world of the Great Spirits, neither here nor there?

Chapter Eight

Ten of us sit around a pile of sizzling hot stones. The oldest grandmother has a face like walnut bark. Mother and I look west, away from the door, so I will not think of leaving before the Spirits find my ear. Little girls pour cold water on the stones to make a sizzling steam rise. So welcome is the steam on my parched body! Minutes pass, maybe hours. The steam saps Mother's energy, and she cannot stay here long. Soon the others leave as well, until I am alone.

My mind travels to other worlds I do not recognize. Images form, foggy and ever changing. I hear the quiet roar of voices, but the words slide past me. They are not in my language and not in the language of my father's people. They are like songs from a different village, riding the wind.

I have heard many stories of men and women who visited our sweat houses, purified their bodies and minds, and received clear messages from the Spirits. I long for just such an experience. I have done everything right—the food, the water, the cleansing of the clutter in my mind, the eternity spent in the steam until I am as limp as the grasses in the marsh—and still I hear nothing to guide me in treating the strange illness that overtakes our people. Nothing.

I am stabbed with disappointment when I leave the sweat house. My head spins as I dive into the stream than runs behind the house, shuddering in the cold waters. Afterward I smear myself with bear's oil and powdered puccoon to seal in the pure cleanliness. I should feel restored by the cold water and the oils, but my energy sags as I trudge up the long hill to the temple. It is as if I am plodding through banks of hot snow, but my anger drives me on. I will tell the priest exactly what troubles my mind. That will salve the wounds of disappointment and cool my anger. Let him explain why the Great Spirits failed me! That is his job, is it not?

The priest smooths his flowing vestments and touches the string of perfect blue-black pearls around his neck. "The Spirits speak to us in their own time," he says.

"Not good enough! I'm ready to hear them now!" I hurl the tobacco leaves as though I am casting poisons into the fire.

"Sacahocan, a sacrifice given in anger is not a sacrifice at all." He thrusts his hand into the fire and scoops up a handful of my leaves. How is he not burned? The leaves drift to the ground, and he directs my eyes to the half-charred pile at my feet. I take a deep, cleansing breath, gather the leaves, and dust them over the fire.

"Better. Now, how may I help you?"

He lowers his jiggling body to the ground, inviting me to sit across from him. He sits very still, waiting for me to speak; I squiggle and squirm in the silence, letting my eyes drift everywhere but to his face. Over there, the statues of our gods and of wolves. There, at the far end of the temple, the platform that holds the decaying bones of our rulers and, under that, a wooden carving of our god Okeus. He is not a kind god, but my mother has told me I must please Okeus, and my rewards will be great. Disappoint Okeus, and my people will be torn by hail and wind, our crops flooded. As if it all falls on my shoulders. "That is what a medicine woman endures," Mother has said many times. "You must understand this if you are to become a *weroansqua* of our people." Mother will never be a full medicine woman, despite her gifts and talents for healing, and she will never be a *weroansqua* because she did the unforgiveable—she married a foreigner. I inherit the rights from my mother, as is the way of our people. Her son would come first, of course, but not Quangatarask. He cannot even get the right moccasin on the right foot.

Now the priest combs his lock with his fingers,

waiting for me to speak. His earring fascinates me – a bear claw. I wonder if the sharp claws stab his cheek when he sleeps. Do priests sleep? Finally the words come to me.

"I must know why our people are dying from a strange illness. And why my mother lived through it when all the others died. And what I can do to heal them. And why I am so angry!"

"Sacahocan, I cannot give you answers to such difficult questions, but this I know. Long ago, before foreigners came to our shores, the prophets foretold of a great blow to our people from invaders. The prophecy has come true. The foreigners have angered the Spirits by heaving our lives out of balance. That is why this dreadful disease spreads among our people, and it will not stop until Okeus is appeased and all is set in harmony again."

"Yes, yes," I eagerly agree. "So what can we do?"

"Ah, not so simple. First the English must be driven from our borders. I wish them no ill," he says gently. "Let them live in peace with their own land and seas, their own king and gods." His voice turns hard and bristly: "They must all leave before the season of budding, before the return of the geese. Every man, woman, and child among them must leave."

I cannot respond. In my heart burns this thought: if my father had left our shores, I would not be here at all.

"The *manito aki* calls for a sacrifice, a perfect child, to save our people from the ravages of the foreigners," the priest continues. "You see that, do you not, Sacahocan?"

Those foggy images in the sweat house, those fuzzy voices just beyond my reach—all begin to clear in my mind. "Yes, a pure offering burned for the gods," I whisper.

"Then the Spirits will push the invaders onto their boats, and they will sail away to distant shores where we will not see them."

Never see another like my father, like me.

"A perfect child, a perfect child," the priest chants. "One gentle, unworldly, unblemished boy, the son of an important woman. Such a child shall be brought to the Great House on the Feast of Nikomis. The smoke and ash that rise from him shall please the gods and our ancestors."

Before the priest speaks again, I know. My heart seizes into an ugly knot as the name comes to his lips:

"On the Feast of Nikomis you will bring the perfect boy to me. Quangatarask shall be the sacrifice."

Chapter Nine

"No!" Mother cries, folding Quangatarask into her arms. He tries to squirm away, but she holds him as tight as if he was still on her cradle board. Quangatarask's father, who has little to do but tend our garden, sits along the wall of our dark house smoking his pipe. If my stomach is the least bit queasy, I gag when his tobacco smoke coils through our *yihakan*.

Now he unfurls his legs and wrenches Quangatarask away from Mother, locking his arm across Little Brother's frail chest. "Think of the honor this worthless bag of bones would bring to our family. He is chosen, wife, the *chosen one*."

"He is not a worthless bag of bones! There is only one in this house." I know the man should send me flying across the house for such hateful words, but Mother steps between us.

Quangatarask loves being the center of our attention. His eyes jump from Mother to me as he curls into his father's lap. I am glad he does not understand the awful things his father says about him.

The evil man turns as sweet as green corn juice. "Daughter—"

"She is not your daughter!" Mother barks.

"Remind me again about the foreigner." He hoists

Quangatarask over his shoulder like a sack of ground corn, and Quangatarask giggles. "I will take him to the priest now."

Mother and I both leap on him, she on the right and I pulling his lock of hair until he cries out and drops Quangatarask to the soft ground.

He growls, "The daughter is just like the mother. I *will* take the boy to the priest when the time is right. You cannot stop me."

Mother says, "I can, husband, if I divorce you. It is my right, and the child stays with me."

My heart rejoices at her words, especially when her husband's face collapses. Without my mother, he would have nothing, and we would have peace.

At that moment a messenger comes. "Rassoum calls for you. Kecuttannowas's leg has snapped like a dry twig. Hurry, Strange Eyes!"

My poor *Lightning!* "My name is Sacahocan," I snap as I clutch my medicine bag and toss a blanket over my shoulders. The day is the first hint of winter. We run to Rassoum's house.

There lies Lightning on a raised platform. A broken bone pokes through his skin like a sharp stick. The cords in Lightning's neck are pulled tight, and he clamps his teeth on the thick tip of his hair lock. A low howl rumbles from his throat.

His eyes greet me with relief. I dab at his forehead with a wet cloth.

Rassoum fires instructions: "Prepare ginger syrup and willow bark oil to ease the pain. Strip two sheets of birch bark clean for splints. Also, find ropes of smooth inner bark to tie the splints in place. Not a minute to waste, Sacahocan."

I hurry to fetch the supplies from the storehouse behind Rassoum's *yihakan*, sick at heart over Lightning's shame. Hunters are not supposed to be injured. Such an injury says more about the cleverness of the prey than it does about the skill of the hunter. But Lightning is in agony. I see in my mind his hands—bloodless, milk white—locked into fists to contain the pain.

When I return, Rassoum is kneading the leg like bread dough. He places my hands on Lightning's leg below his left knee. "Do you feel where the bone is strong, here? And here, where it is weak?" I close my eyes and let my hands see. Yes! "Ease the jagged piece into place like this, Sacahocan." My fingers follow his. Lightning's whole body tightens like a taut rope. The pain storm must be torrential. A trickle of blood oozes out of his mouth where he's bitten his tongue.

When we have worked the bone into place, Rassoum wraps the leg in birch bark and firmly ties the splint around the straight leg. "Now, Sacahocan?"

What do I tell Lightning? "Do not put any weight on this leg for three days."

"Seven," Rassoum says.

"Yes. In seven days your brothers will carry you back here to see how the leg is healing. Rassoum will give you medicines to ease the pain."

"What more?" my teacher urges.

"In a moon's time you will toddle like a baby just learning to walk or like an old man. In another moon your leg will heal, and then you must give thanks that all is in harmony again."

Lightning nods, too pained to speak.

"The girl is wise," Rassoum says. "Now, sleep." Lightning gratefully closes his eyes against the torment. The medicines make him drowsy. Soon his breaths come long and steady, the pain buried deep in his mind.

"Ah, the comfort of sleep," Rassoum says, taking up his pipe as his reward for a job done as the Spirits would wish. I, only 13 summers, am not allowed to smoke. I watch him enviously, promising that when I become *weroansqua* of this tribe, girls will certainly be allowed to smoke a pipe!

When Lightning wakes, Rassoum busies himself at

the far side of the house. Like everyone else, he knows that Lightning expects me to be his wife. "Brave warrior," our villagers often taunt, "willing to take on a vixen like Strange Eyes." I am not such a vixen now when I sit Lightning up and give him spoonfuls of sweetened corn mush dotted with dried grapes.

"How did this happen?" I ask. Afternoon sunlight streams in through the open door, setting Lightning's handsome face in a half shadow.

"I crept up on a family of rabbits. Slowly I moved my arm to throw a net over all of them. One spied me, warned the others, and they ran off. I couldn't let them escape—all those white pelts would make a fine coat for you, and there would be tasty stew enough for our whole village. I chased them deep into the forest."

"Yes?" I wait for the heroic part that is sure to follow—a leap off a cliff, an encounter with a hungry brown bear.

Lightning's eyes turn away. "I tripped over a fallen log."

"You tripped? Opechancanough's greatest hunter *tripped* over a fallen log?" I laugh and laugh.

"Don't. It hurts," but he laughs anyway and says, "When we are married, Sacahocan, we will laugh every day."

At that moment I think it would not be terrible to

have such a man for a husband, but in a moment, the feeling could billow like smoke. It has always been like this between Lightning and me.

"You will be a great medicine woman. Our people will travel from far-off villages to place themselves in your healing hands. I will be the proudest husband in all of Chief Powhatan's empire."

Yes, it is sounding better and better, but one worry nags at me. "And what of Little Brother?" I do not tell Lightning what the high priest intends for Quangatarask during the winter Feast of Nikomis. Putting it in words would make the horror too real to bear.

What shoots from Lightning's mouth is almost as bad: "When your mother grows too old to care for him, Quangatarask can live with a woman who has no husband and no children to bother her."

My blood streams cold despite the fire behind me. All the ease of the past moments rises with the smoke in the *yihakan*. "As long as Quangatarask lives, he lives with me."

"Pah!" Lightning says. "If he's not eaten by wolves, he'll be a child in a man's body. There is no room in my house for him."

I sit up, the bones in my back as straight as a broom. "Then there is no room in your house for me.

I will call for your brothers to carry you home." I leave him sputtering, and—Ahone, god of creation, forgive me—I no longer care if Lightning suffers pain from the snapping of his leg or from the breaking of his cold heart.

Chapter Ten

"Cor-o-na-shun, yes, the foreigners finally recognize our greatness!" someone yells around the campfire.

All of my worries about Little Brother must be put aside, for our whole village is going to Werowocomoco. Also a thousand of our neighbors—the Kecoughtan and the Paspahegh and the Chickahominy—all of us in our great empire. I do not understand the custom, but the English king has decided to honor Powhatan, our Great Chief, by giving him a crown of great beauty and worth. The ceremony is called a cor-o-na-shun, a word my father never taught me. The word buzzes all over our village.

"Pah, cor-o-na-shun is a trick to make us English."

"To steal more of our land." Many agree.

"Cor-o-na-shun makes Powhatan as important as their king." Fewer agree.

"At least it will mean a day of feasting!" That we all rejoice in, for a lean time looms ahead with the snows.

Deer Knife brings back word that more than a hundred people from the Jamestown Colony will be going to Werowocomoco. Will Ly-iss be among them? I will take some of our herbs and roots to share with him, and I will ask him for help with our sick and dying. Mother is still weak, and I fear that the disease will overtake her again. She is not hearty enough to walk with us to Werowocomoco.

The festival begins at dawn. Painted and feathered, shod in fragrant new moccasins and warmed by deerskin mantles, we all gather at the great house of Chief Powhatan. Never have I seen a bigger *yihakan!* Twenty of my mother's houses could fit in that one. Powhatan men sit on benches along the south wall, women along the north wall, but we guests are seated at the feet of the Great Chief in half circles, tribe by tribe, men and women together. The English perch closest to Powhatan, for they have the jeweled crown and a hundred other gifts for our chief.

Fortune is with me this beautiful morning—my people are led to the row right behind the English, so I will not miss a word that is spoken, in both my languages. But the waves of odor from their unwashed bodies send my head reeling. In my pouch is a tincture of goldenrod in case any of my people faint from the stench. I breathe through my mouth to chase the smell away.

There in the English circle I spot a head full of wild curls, nearly the color of the deer hair we dye red. I slide around in the circle to sit right behind

Ly-iss. I tap his shoulder, and he nearly jumps out of his pale, pale skin! "Shh," I tell him, "and do not stand up until the chief tells us to." His springy curls dance around as the speeches begin—and go on and on and on. When his head droops to his shoulder, I poke him to wake him up. He turns around and smiles his open-faced grin. Is it necessary to show everything you feel right on your face? Our people guard their faces better.

Chief Powhatan calls for Nantaquod, his name for Ly-iss's father, the *weroance* of the foreigners, but Nantaquod is not here, and I am glad. There are rumbles in our many languages about his rudeness—what could be more important than this day?

So, with their *weroance* absent, Chief Powhatan demands that his son come forward, and Ly-iss stumbles to his feet to stand beside the great chief. I watch his knees knock and his face turn the color of mulberries. People all around me chuckle—until Chief Powhatan calls for the youngest woman present. With the chant of "Strange Eyes, Strange Eyes," I am pushed forward to stand beside the chief, facing Ly-iss.

What do I read in Ly-iss's eyes? Fear? Maybe he thinks this is to be his last day on earth, and it could be, for Chief Powhatan is known to have a cruel streak, preying on weakness. I try to send Ly-iss a signal: *None of that foreigner's joking; close your face the way my people do, so there is no door or window open to your soul.*

We wash and dry our hands, and then I am startled by a blast from a musical instrument, much like the cry of a wounded deer. Now the different English *weroance* speaks, then our chief, then the foreigner, then our chief, and each tries to sound more important and more powerful than the other. I must guard my face so as not to show the amusement that is bubbling in my throat. My feet play with lumps of earth under my moccasins, my fingers with beads on my medicine pouch. My stomach growls, and I can smell the feast awaiting us beyond the *yihakan*. Will we ever be done with this cor-o-na-shun?

The foreigner tries to place the jeweled crown on our chief's head, but he cannot reach, and the chief will not kneel or lower his head to allow the crown. Another try and another try, but it is hopeless. But the Chief loves the attention and the gifts—like Quangatarask!

I cannot read Ly-iss's face, except for the impatience that propels him forward to actually touch, *push* the Chief's head! Is he crazy? Our people will rise up against him!

But in an instant the English *weroance* locks the crown firmly over Chief Powhatan's head, and the Chief grins, signaling us to forgive the foreigners and to rejoice in their innocent foolishness on this happy day. A great cry of celebration goes up among the English, and our drums begin their rhythmic pounding. Chants in a dozen languages fill the house as people march in with pots and platters heaped with food. I fill a plate and slip away, too shocked to talk to Ly-iss.

Touching the Chief without permission? Men have been executed for less.

Chapter Eleven

Deer Knife is digging out a canoe that will hold 20 hunters. He is not a great hunter himself. When he was a boy no bigger than Quangatarask, he poked a stick in one ear to see if he could make it come out the other ear. He must have thought our heads were full of moss! I remember his cries of agony that echoed all over our village when he popped something inside his head. Rassoum says it was like making a hole in the skin of a drum, after which the sound from the drum is as weak as a sigh. Since that day no sound goes in Deer Knife's left ear, so we all speak to the right of him, and he hears us well enough. But how can a man be a great hunter if his two ears do not pick up the quiet sounds of the forest, the skittering of opossums and raccoons? Deer come on padded feet over soft pine needles. An angry stag, grieving for his dead mate, could suddenly appear behind Deer Knife and attack with a full rack of horns. That is how Deer Knife got his name—the stag was like a knife wounding his pride. Somehow he survived *huskanaw*. Lightning and the other young hunters take Deer Knife on the hunts, but they must be his ears. What he lacks in his ear he makes up for with a sharp eye for prey and a steady arm, and so his arrows shoot straight and far.

Deer Knife has told me his secret: that he has little appetite for killing animals, and that makes him as strange to our people as I am.

Still, a people must have builders and artists as well as hunters. Deer Knife does not need good ears to carve and scrape and paint, and so his canoes are works of art—beautiful and watertight and nearly unsinkable.

I watch him carve away tree flesh, his skin sweaty from the fire in the center of the tree that will become a flat-bottom canoe. It is nearly as deep as I am tall.

"Sacahocan!" he says merrily, grinning and wiping sweat from his brow with the back of his arm. His hair lock is wound around his head so it will not fly into the fire. "How is the little man?"

"Oh, he fell into the river while I was at Werowocomoco, but at least that worthless father of his fished him out."

"His father must teach him to swim," Deer Knife says.

How? And why, I wonder, if the sweet child is to be given in sacrifice, but I do not mention this to Deer Knife. The Feast of Nikomis is only weeks away, deep in the heart of the season of cohonks, and I am helpless to save Quangatarask.

Scritch-scritch. I remember how this scraping of

the shell against the wood hurts my teeth.

Deer Knife hops out of the canoe and pulls a deerskin over his back. As soon as he is away from the fire, the biting cold will freeze the sweat on his shoulders. I am glad to have the scritching stop. We sit on the ground, huddled in our mantles. A sad feeling sweeps over me, as if something terrible is about to happen.

Deer Knife says, "Later today I will come to your *yihakan* with three big fish."

Does this mean . . . ? "What kind of fish?" I ask.

"I don't know. I haven't speared them yet!"

I smile. "My mother favors widemouthed bass, but she would not turn away plump, juicy sturgeon."

"And would you turn me away?" he asks shyly.

How to answer? "That depends on how large the fish are."

He glances at me out of the corner of his eyes, and this is enough of an answer. For now.

"What was that, Deer Knife?" I point. He has not heard the sounds of something streaking through the forest, quick as a rabbit but tall as a man. We jump to our feet to chase the thing in the forest, Deer Knife with his knife unsheathed in case of danger.

There behind a yellow pine a head pokes out, and two wide eyes stare at us, their terror clear. What sort of animal has blue eyes? I creep closer, and the animal darts away, as swift and graceful as a young deer, but it is not a deer. It is a boy with yellow hair and blue eyes, ragged and barefoot, and now he has disappeared into the forest.

"Did you see what I saw?" Deer Knife asks.

"A foreign boy, yes."

"From the English colony."

"No. Did you see his clothes?"

"From where, then?"

"I do not know," I whisper, but I do know. He is another like me, a child of the foreigners who came with my father, but all of his people are gone, and he has been living like a wild animal in the forest for many seasons, alone, alone.

Later, at sundown, my heart is still heavy with thoughts of the foreign boy when Deer Knife taps on our door, bearing a large covered basket. Mother welcomes him, and Quangatarask leaps into his arms, but I hang back along the wall admiring how comely he looks, with his face painted the red of bloodroot and dusted with fine yellow sparkles. His hair lock is clean and sleekly black, combed with hickory oil. A few feathers in his knot flutter in the breeze.

"Come in," Mother says, closing the deerskin door

against the cold. She leads him to our fire and scoops out a bowl of corn mush for him, sweetened with mulberries and crunchy walnuts.

He sits by the fire, with Quangatarask still clamped to his hip. Mother glances over at me to show she approves. Deer Knife lifts the cover on the basket and presents three fat fish with silvery scales and fins and eyes as black as coal. Suddenly, Quangatarask's father is interested, scooping the fish into his arms like returning relatives. He looks at me, looks at Deer Knife.

"Ah!" he says, understanding that Deer Knife gives these gifts as a marriage proposal. Quangatarask's father is only too glad to marry me off! I can see the thoughts clicking through his head: *First the boy goes to the Great Spirits, and then the girl goes to Deer Knife's yihakan, and I am left in peace!*

At that moment a gust of wind blows the deerskin door flap open. A wind devil curls through our house and aims right for the fire. We are plunged into darkness. The fire that burns in a Pamunkee house day and night, never to be extinguished, has died in the wind. Mother quickly tries to rekindle the fire by rubbing a pointed stick against a dry-wood starter, but it is too late. Each of us, even Quangatarask's father, knows that the dying of the flames is an evil omen.

Chapter Twelve

Scouts bring back information: the foreigners have no food for the winter. They hoped the cor-o-na-shun would soften Chief Powhatan's heart, but it has done the opposite.

Opechancanough stands on a high platform, with Lightning leaning on a thick branch on one side of him, favoring his mending leg, and Deer Knife proud on the other. Our *weroance* seems as tall as the gods, and we stretch our necks to see each line of his face as Opechancanough announces, "The English, the furry ones, the thieves of our land, will come begging. By order of my brother, the Great Chief Powhatan, we shall not trade with them."

A great cheer rises, which Quangatarask joins, perched on his father's shoulders.

Someone shouts, "Let the beasts starve and die away."

"Not a kernel of corn!" another man yells.

The crowd falls silent with just the raising of Opechancanough's hand. "When they come with their miserly beads and copper and scissors and thread and their empty barges, we will give them more than they ask for."

An anxious silence veils the crowd.

"We will release our arrows into each man who comes ashore, and any that survive shall be peeled like skin from a plum. We shall fill their empty barges with their ashes!"

"Yes!" everyone cries, even Deer Knife, even my mother. Does she forget that she once loved my father?

It pains me that Quangatarask hears such merciless talk. I tap his father's shoulder. "Let me take him home," I beg, though I rarely speak words aloud to him anymore.

He lets Quangatarask slide down his flank, and I edge our way through the crowd.

"Little Brother, tomorrow we go to see Ly-iss." My promise sounds light and hearty, but worry worms into my heart. Tomorrow will be the first time since Lightning killed their man to avenge Cougar. Maybe Ly-iss will not welcome me.

Tonight I will plead with our *weroances* not to stoop to the level of the foreigners, slaughtering innocents so callously. But if they will not listen, I must warn the English. They are my people too.

Before the sun turns the sky pink and orange I awaken Quangatarask, with my finger on my lips to remind him to be quiet. Behind the curtain, our mother and her husband sleep; his snores ripple the curtain.

All is ready for our journey.

Outside our village I tell Quangatarask, "You must walk the whole way yourself. I can barely lift you anymore." He trots a mile or two until the sun is full yellow in the eastern sky and then begs to travel on my back.

It is the season of cohonks. "Honk-honk!" Quangatarask mimics the two geese flying overhead. They are scouts looking for a good place for their flock to winter, just as our hunters send scouts to find the richest winter hunting grounds.

Quangatarask and I sing as we walk: "You are a clever hunter, and your people's young will tell of your bravery for one hundred seasons." Little Brother loves the song, not guessing that he will never be a clever hunter, but why spoil a boy's dreaming? And besides, the melody lightens the heavy load of Quangatarask on my shoulders and the treachery of my people on my mind.

Treachery? Who is the traitor here? Such strange days we live in.

We sing the song a thousand times until we near the foreigners' camp. "Hush, Quangatarask. We mustn't scare their dogs and horses." I do not tell him how frightened I am to be walking into the enemy's camp. Just two nights earlier, around our fire, I had heard Opitchapam, another of our *weroances*, tell about a battle between our warriors and the English.

"They have no business being on our land, aye? We rushed in before dawn and took them by surprise," he said with pride. "Before they found their weapons we'd shot three men and pulled our arrows out of their hides to use them again on worthier prey. It was beautiful! One prancing chicken we took hostage."

"Ai-ai-ai! Still in his nightclothes, with a trapdoor that opened on his behind!" Blackbear strutted around the fire, pretending to unbutton his clothing to show his own backside. This brought riotous laughter to all of us, but then the mood turned serious again as Opitchapam said, "We were two miles upriver when we spotted them coming toward us in their flat-bottom boat. 'Duck,' I shouted, just as their bullets began to whistle through the air."

Blackbear finished the story: "Our *weroance* was very clever. He held the white man up in front of him like a sack stuffed full of straw."

"The perfect target," Opitchapam said boastfully. "And not one of our men had so much as a burn of a bullet flying by because every bullet lodged in the white man's body. He's now floating in the bay. Food for the fish, aye?"

"Next spring we'll catch some of those fattened fish!" one of the warriors said, and the rest of them took up the chant: "Next spring . . . Next spring . . ."

Now, as we near the foreigners' camp, I think of those bullets sailing by from the powerful fire sticks. I see the men standing guard at the top of their palisade wall. "Very quiet, Quangatarask, promise?"

"I promise!" he shouts, running ahead.

I hear a rustling along the barrier of the fort. Then one of the men says, "It's just that Indian girl and her idiot brother."

Another says, "Could be decoys. Could be a whole tribe of savages hanging back behind her."

"Stand ready, men. Guns ready."

Just put one foot in front of the other, I tell myself, holding Quangatarask's arm in a grip that will raise a bruise. And hold your head up proudly. Yet how can I be proud? I am walking into the enemy camp to place my own people in danger at the hands of those who are . . . also my people.

Chapter Thirteen

"Ly-iss!" Quangatarask cries, running ahead of me into the fort. Ly-iss is cutting the hair of a man who sits on a tree stump, and why, I cannot guess. The hair barely reaches the foreigner's shoulders. Ly-iss should be cutting the ugly beard instead!

Our men, of course, pluck the hairs from around their foreheads and from over their right ears so they will not get in the way of a quiver of arrows or a taut bow drawn to fire. Over their left shoulders hang long knots of beautiful dark hair.

Ly-iss drops his cutting tool as Quangatarask rushes forward and flattens himself on Ly-iss like a jellyfish on the bottom of a canoe.

He pats Quangatarask's head and smiles. His teeth are yellow and not straight like rows of corn. Also, his skin is mottled and red. Does he have the sickness of Graywolf and my mother? No. He crackles with energy as he carries Quangatarask to the place where the foreigners' horses live. Its strange door is split in half across, so the top half swings open while the bottom half stays shut. Quangatarask climbs on the bottom door and hangs his head and shoulders inside. He and the horses talk like old friends, but Ly-iss and I stumble over every word. I have not used the

English of my father in many years. I used to practice it in my head when I was falling asleep, but with no one to say the words aloud to, how can I be sure I speak them properly? And I have such an important message for the foreigners. Unspoken between us is the grief of the killings on both sides, like a bear sleeping in your *yihakan* that everyone dares not wake.

"Ly-iss, I have heard that your people come to my village to trade for food. Tell your father, your *weroance*. Tell him not to come."

Ly-iss thinks I am making a joke. He laughs so easily and sometimes forgets when to be serious. My father was also like that.

I pull my forehead into a frown, hoping he will understand what I cannot say. "There is danger. No more can I tell you."

All my life Mother has taught me about loyalty. "You must stand by the people who love you, daughter, even if they do not show their love, and you will find that the Spirits will be loyal to you and send healing through your hands to our people."

Her words fill my head, like voices across the water, but now my mind whirls in confusion: loyalty I understand but to which side? "Just promise me, promise me," I beg Ly-iss.

So Ly-iss promises to warn the chief, but it will not help. He is like me in many ways—part of his people and yet apart.

I wonder if the foreigners suffer the same fever and red itchy bumps that plague my people and if they will live to enjoy another planting season. I mention all of this to Ly-iss.

"Pox, measles. Yes, we're overrun with them," Ly-iss tells me. He fills a beautiful tortoise shell with medicines for when this sickness comes, some to drink, some to rub on the red bumps. This part is horrible: he and his medicine man cut the feverish patient to let bad blood trickle out. I shudder at the picture in my mind: Mother's trusting eyes look up at me as the fever and headache pounded through her. How could I be so cruel as to cut into a person raging with fever? How can a person's blood, his life-feeding water, be bad? But Ly-iss tells me that many of his people survive this sickness.

"I will use your remedies and our own together," I tell Ly-iss, and he will do the same.

We are friends, Ly-iss and I, although his people and mine are enemies. And tomorrow the English will come to my village. I am afraid a river of blood will flow. "Promise to warn them," I say again, and his eyes finally show that he understands the danger. No more joking.

The days are short, and the sky threatens snow. Little Brother and I begin the long journey home, although he does not want to leave Ly-iss or the horses. I think the horses are lonely, like Quangatarask. The forest is silent. Many animals have gone to their warm shelters for the winter. Little Brother grows sleepy, and I drape him across my shoulders the way the hunters bring home deer. Soon he will be eight summers—12 summers—and what then, when I can no longer carry him?

As flakes of snow drift onto my face, my pace quickens, and then a shocking thought gallops through my head: this strange new sickness that takes my people away from us, while the foreigners survive it? It is not the angry Spirits that are making us sick. The English themselves have brought this disease to our shores and made our people sick! And have we spread our diseases to them? Is *this* how the Spirits set all in balance?

I've trudged all the way back to Menapacute, wanting only sleep, but our three *weroances*, brothers of the Great Chief Powhatan, call us together on this frosty evening. Opitchapam stands to the right, Kekataugh to the left, and Opechancanough in the center, tall as a pine. They are three parts of a leaf, ruling as one, but we all know which is the stem that holds the leaf together.

Now Opechancanough speaks, and his voice is a bear roar: "The barbarians are too lazy to farm, too clumsy to hunt, and too stupid to preserve what food they have for the winter. Tomorrow the helpless beasts will come begging to us."

"In trade," Opitchapam reminds his brother.

"Pah, a few beads! We ask them for guns, they bring us needles and thread or a hatchet or two if they're hungry enough."

Kekataugh, who is always thirsty for war, says, "We can pick them off with arrows as they set foot on the shore."

"No, let's give them a few bushels of corn and send them back to the water," Opitchapam says. "Let them go to the Nasamond or their lucky neighbors, the Paspahegh, and cheat *them* out of winter stores. We have little enough for ourselves."

Men all around argue these points. The air is charged, like before a great hurricane. They are calling for foreign blood but do not consider that blood will be shed on both sides of the battle. It is an honor to die in a noble war, of course, but no honor to drag wounded bodies home. Those they leave to Rassoum and me to mend.

Opechancanough hushes the crowd. "This is what we will do." He turns to his brothers, who nod their agreement. "We'll kill them with kindness." He grins, a smile without joy. "They'll be our honored guests. We'll load their barges with our best corn. Afterward we'll invite them to feast and dance with us and sleep by the fire."

A grumbling protest goes up.

"Silence! Hear me out. When they're fattened and weak from dancing into the night, we'll unload the barges and take back our corn!"

The crowd goes wild with joy, and my heart is sucked under like sand at high tide. We Pamunkee are free to enter anyone's house and scoop from the pot that is always cooking over their fire, and we are trusted never to take anything from their house that is not ours. "But stealing from the enemy is fair," Mother always says, and this is the only thing she teaches me that I doubt.

That is not the worst of it for this night.

Opechancanough raises his hand to quiet us. "So, when the woolly beasts have put down their fire sticks and drifted into sleep, we'll creep into their tent and slaughter them, one and all, with their own guns!"

Chapter Fourteen

The foreigners are here now, and Ly-iss is among them. Our eyes meet across the crowd, and a smile of hope brightens his face. Knowing what his fate is, I cannot return the smile, and then I see his smile die and a blush rise in his cheeks. His father hits the side of Ly-iss's head to remind him to listen to Chief Opechancanough.

The feasting begins, the dancing, and the good cheer that each side pretends is real. I look at these strange lumbering men, with their beards and hats, holey boots, and sheathed swords and fire sticks. Someday I will be a Dream-Reader—that is what I have decided—and perhaps I will learn to read the foreigners' dreams.

I crouch outside their tent, waiting for the rhythms of sleep. I will not read their dreams this night, and they may never dream again. Soon our warriors will be surrounding the tent in a silent dance.

Now! This is my last chance to slip inside.

Ly-iss is the smallest lump under the deerskin blankets. "Leave, out!" I whisper. "They watch 'til you grow drowsy with food and drink. Then they will kill you. Kill you, Ly-iss!" I push his medicine bag into his arms. "Go!"

They do not believe me. Their *weroance* says, "Ignore the girl."

Ly-iss begs his father to trust my words. One of the English clutches his fire stick, and the *weroance* shouts, "Fire!"

I jump away from the gun. He shoots straight up into the smoke hole—to warn others or to scare our warriors? The thunder deafens my ears, but I am grateful still to be standing.

Lightning always tells me that the English are cowards, and now I see it with my own eyes. I have risked my life for people who respect themselves so little that they now slither out of the tent like snakes.

I peek outside. Deer Knife is closest among the warriors towering over the serpents. Even Lightning is there, his weight resting on his good leg. All of the men have bows drawn. They have been told not to shoot. *Why?* Opechancanough must have other, more terrible plans for them.

Now the English *weroance* orders his men to stand and walk with dignity. Too late. Ly-iss totters to his feet, glances back—looking for me?—and walks behind his father. I hear the heavy footsteps of other foreigners coming our way. Blood will muddy the good earth beneath our feet. Is *this* what pleases the Spirits?

But living among warriors has taught me well. Just when my heart is softened toward our enemy, for all blood is the same color, a tree whooshes into flames, and the flames tear from tree to tree until they torch the first house. That house is ashes in minutes, and its sparks ignite the next house. The sky burns orange at midnight, the heat searing deerskin, corn, and human flesh.

The English have set fire to our whole village!

Warriors are meant to fall in battle, but with a fire storm, women and children also burn. Chief Opechancanough is right. The English *are* barbarians.

Seven have died, including Cougar's grieving mother. Rage sweeps me away in its flood, and I am as bloodthirsty as our warriors. *Revenge!* my black heart sings.

Quangatarask's father organizes the burials. Many others—Pamunkee and one English—writhe on mats out in the open path between our houses. Rassoum and I hurry from mat to mat, peeling away charred flesh. In my rage I must remind myself to be gentle as I wash and dress the skin beneath that is as red as fresh meat.

Oh! Quangatarask's little arm is seared. His whimpers break my heart, my blackened heart.

Mother harvests her sagging energy to comfort Little Brother and a dozen others. Mercifully, they're gone, the foreigners.

But then Ly-iss's father tears into the clearing, dragging Chief Opechancanough by his hair lock and pressing a gun to his back. How can he humiliate our *weroance* this way, especially after causing such suffering among our people? The foreigners are without decency! He commands Opechancanough to reload bushels of corn onto the English barges. Opechancanough refuses, showing no pain, no fear, despite the gun now aimed at his right eye.

Then I am sure that Ly-iss's father is a monster more vicious than any beast of the forest.

Those of us still standing hear Opechancanough shout an order that satisfies the monster who does not know our language: "Give them six bushels of corn, each ear dipped in the latrine." Our men run to do his bidding.

Terror streaks across Ly-iss's face. He looks at me, and I turn my eyes away. His father notices one of his English lying apart from our people. Jerking Opechancanough by the hair, he stumbles over.

"George?"

The foreigner weakly replies, "Aye. Me and an Indian knife had a sharp difference of opinion. G'wan without me, Captain. I've shed more blood than whot

I come with. Tell Bones I didn't wash away in a river or nothin', eh?"

Nodding, the English *weroance* backs away, still dragging Opechancanough with a gun to his head until they disappear in the forest. A blind arrow whirs across the air, and then so many arrows fly that the English coward flees. Chief Opechancanough is returned to us, swearing revenge as he marches toward his *yihakan*. I sense his deep shame.

Ly-iss moves toward me. His eyes fall upon Quangatarask and the charred flesh near Little Brother's wrist. He snaps open his medical pouch and smears a foreign paste on the burn. The sweet smell does not fool me.

"Leave him alone!" I scream, tearing the jar out of his hands and tossing it into the bushes.

"It's best for burns," Ly-iss says. "Trust me."

Why should I trust him? He is one of *them*, who follow no rules of warfare, who slaughter women and children.

Ly-iss forages in the bushes for his jar of burn paste. Rassoum watches Ly-iss dart from mat to mat, ripping holes in the knees of his breeches. He is slathering our people's burn wounds with that strange English paste. And then he sees the foreigner and rushes over to tend to his wound that is pumping blood. Taking a curved needle out of his pouch, Ly-iss bites his lip as he hits his friend with a rock to knock him out. "Otherwise he couldn't stand the pain," he quickly explains. Rassoum signals for me to watch closely as Ly-iss licks the thread and makes tiny, even stitches. He is a thread artist, just as Deer Knife is a canoe artist. Rassoum watches in wonder, his own fingers following Ly-iss, stitch by stitch.

I set a crock of our burn remedy on the ground beside Ly-iss and hope he will understand that I am trying to forgive him for what his people have done to mine, but it is not easy. I tell myself, *He is not like them, just as my father was not like them.*

Chapter Fifteen

We Pamunkee are not a people easily defeated. In defiance of the English our women are rebuilding the houses after the fire, and our men are plotting revenge. I see no end to this warfare unless the foreigners sail away. How can so gentle a soul as Ly-iss belong to such a cruel and warring people?

This thought haunts me as Rassoum and I attend the sick and burned, stealing moments of sleep when we can. So it is a joy when Deer Knife says, "Quangatarask and I are going fishing. It's a clear day. We'll have no trouble breaking through the thin ice to find fish." He has gotten Mother's blessing for this outing.

"Be careful with Little Brother. A log at least floats when it falls from the tree. Quangatarask sinks. He can't remember to kick his feet and move his arms at the same time."

Deer Knife gives me a shy look. "You could come with us, Sacahocan. Two paddlers would move us faster through the water."

I would not be alone with Deer Knife, and I would be able to watch Little Brother when he's flailing around in the canoe. "I suppose I could go, if Rassoum does not need me."

Deer Knife beams with pleasure. He has no little brother to tend, for he is the youngest of his mother's four children. And Quangatarask needs a friend, someone other than me and the English boy a world away.

At the river Deer Knife balances the canoe on his head and his gleaming locust bow, like no one else's, on his shoulder. In his pouch are fishhooks fashioned from the small, hollow tails of crabs, chinaroot powder for quick food, and, of course, hunters go nowhere without magical tobacco.

My medicine pouch hangs around my neck, anchored by Quangatarask's moccasins, for he rides on my shoulders. On cloudless days I have caught my reflection in the water. Then I see hair clean and wavy, the markings on my arms and neck vibrant in blues and reds and yellows. But my shoulders? Not pretty. They've grown as broad as a bench since I am the beast that Little Brother rides. His father says, "Pah, with shoulders like that, no man will be able to get his arms around you."

I want to shout at him, "My life's purpose is not hunting a husband to hold me!" but I bite my tongue, for my people teach respect even for elders who do not earn respect.

Now Quangatarask's head droops onto mine, and I

hear his sweet mewls of sleep, so it is safe to talk to Deer Knife. Test him, a little.

"Today the clouds let Father Sun shine through to warm our backs, but tonight we'll be shivering under our furs. Soon it will be time for the Grandmother's Dance at the Feast of Nikomis."

"I'll be ready!" Deer Knife has been gathering otter pelts for his arms and eagle feathers for his headdress and grinding bloodroot and wild indigo into red and blue powders to paint his face. He is one of the hunters who have just come through *huskanaw*, and it is their honor to lead the men of the tribe in the dancing. Lightning is one among them, but I do not know if he will dance. I remember him hiding away, carving the wolf's head, and I think of his broken leg slowly mending. My heart begins to melt. Then I remember how angry he makes me, and my heart again turns to stone.

We move along. The path is clearer now that the trees have shed, but our feet sink into leaves sodden with snow. I steal a glance at Deer Knife, with his arms raised to support the canoe. He is not as pleasing to the eye as Lightning is. He is only a hand's width taller than I am. His face is pitted and his shoulders rounded, as though he is always on the way to pick something up.

"Deer Knife, may I speak honestly?"

His eyes dance.

"At the Feast of Nikomis a child will be sacrificed to the Spirits. A pure, unblemished child."

"Yes, that is the way of our people."

Crunch-crunch. My feet grind the snow to powder. "The honor has fallen to my family."

Deer Knife jerks his head toward Little Brother, the question looming in his dark eyes.

I nod miserably.

He says nothing for one or two minutes and then repeats, "It's the way of our people."

"But Quangatarask won't understand! And I can't bear the thought. How could the Spirits be so cruel as to take a sweet innocent like Little Brother?"

"Ours is not to question, Sacahocan. Let's keep walking."

Foolish me. I thought he would help me run away to another tribe. Swim to an island where Quangatarask would be safe. Find the lost colony of my father's people.

Can we escape the Great Spirits? Hide where they cannot see us? Do they have eyes everywhere and arms pulling Little Brother ever closer to the fire? I shift his weight. His head jerks up just as I pass under the jagged branches of a bare oak.

"Aieeeee!" Quangatarask cries.

"What? WHAT?" I bend so he can slide down over my head. Blood pours down his face. "Deer Knife, look!"

He drops the canoe down and lifts Quangatarask. Blood spurts all over Deer Knife's mantle. Little Brother screams at a pitch that makes my ears throb. I tear open my medical pouch, murmuring prayers and recalling the steps Rassoum has taught me. I stop the bleeding long enough to see that I will need to sew Quangatarask back together, or he will have a gaping wound that will not heal and will be food for maggots. If only I could sew as well as Ly-iss!

Deer Knife holds Quangatarask to keep him down. He thrashes and wails piteously as I clean and sew the gash with thin threads of deer sinew, reminding myself that I must treat this wound as I would one on any other patient and not think of him as the brother I love more than life.

When it is over, brown stitches track down his face from his left eye to his chin. Without a word, Deer Knife and I reverse our path and walk back to the village, but I carry Quangatarask in my arms. I've given him herbs to ease his pain, and finally he sleeps fitfully. "Poor, sweet Quangatarask." My voice is thick with unspent tears.

I see that Deer Knife weighs whether he should speak. Taking in a deep breath, he says, "Your brother is no longer suitable for the the Feast of Nikomis."

The stitches! Why did I not think of this solution myself? And yet how could I bear to hurt sweet Quangatarask deliberately? But it's done now, and my heart leaps with a curious mix of joy and sorrow. My arms are full of Little Brother; I cannot dry the tears streaming down my face.

Deer Knife is embarrassed by my tears and walks ahead of us and then returns when I have composed myself. "Sacahocan, I have spoken to your mother."

Oh! He means more than just *speaking*.

He gently takes Quangatarask from my arms and places the little round head on his own broad shoulder.

"Be careful of the wound," I caution, my heart racing.

"Your brother is my brother," Deer Knife says. "When we make our own *yihakan* far away from our parents' homes, Quangatarask's mat and bowl will be with ours."

How I've longed to hear such words from Lightning, and now they fall from Deer Knife's lips? I must watch what I say. No promises, but also, I must not bury a path I might need to cross later.

"Not too far from my mother's house or Rassoum's. We three work together until I have learned everything I must to be a medicine woman."

The only sound between us is the brush and snow that we flatten with our moccasins and Quangatarask's small snores. Deer Knife's silence unnerves me. We pass an endless blur of bare trees before he speaks.

"The woman I marry will cook the fish she catches, sew the clothes we wear, pound powders into dyes for our skins, and teach our sons to shoot a bow and arrow."

"Yes." *What more?*

He clears a froggy sound from his throat and squares his shoulders. Quangatarask bounces along, blanketed by Deer Knife's hair lock. "The woman I marry will not be a medicine woman."

I bristle at his thorny words. "Then who is the woman you will marry?"

"I told you. I have spoken to your mother."

"But you have not spoken to me until now, and the words I hear I do not like."

Chapter Sixteen

"I will not marry Deer Knife!" I shout.

"And why not?" Mother's lips are twisted in disapproval. She's weaving a tall basket, one of many for my wedding. Quangatarask's father is out digging graves. He has finally found his place in our village, but his is a job without dignity, and it suits him perfectly. Quangatarask has gone with him to examine the clods of dirt he loves.

"Two suitors my daughter has. Lightning is a handsome hunter and a good provider," Mother reminds me.

My heart sighs. "He only wants to brag, 'I am the husband of the medicine woman!' He wants me because he thinks I will bring him honor someday, and he doesn't want Little Brother at all."

"Hmmm," Mother says, swiftly braiding even rows of red and green straw.

"I will *not* marry Lightning either!"

"Pah! You will grow old alone."

Alone is better than the husband you live with, I think, but I will not hurt her feelings. "Maybe I'll marry someday, Mother, but for now, I've made up my mind to go to Werowocomoco. The Dream-Reader who saved your life welcomes me as his student."

"So far away, daughter?" Mother's face sinks in sadness. "Quangatarask and I will miss you."

"I would like to take Little Brother with me. He's such a comfort at the bedside of sick people, calming them as I listen to their dreams. He's happy to cuddle up next to anyone who's kind to him."

"And leave me alone?" Mother says sharply.

"Not alone. There is—" I so rarely speak his real name "—Arrokoth. He'll be happier if Quangatarask and I are both gone."

Mother says nothing but sets the basket aside, with the unwoven straw waving across her face. *Hiding tears?* "It is only a two-day walk. You will come home for the festivals?"

"Yes!"

"And my birthday?"

"Of course."

"And to visit the bones of your father?" she whispers.

"Yes."

Mother nods, and it is settled, but I know her heart is rock heavy. After a time she takes up the weaving again and says, "Deer Knife will be very disappointed. Pah! He is too short for you."

Quangatarask is excited about our adventures ahead

in Werowocomoco. "You will be the medicine boy," I promise him. We are hurrying to leave before the Feast of Nikomis. Another family has been chosen for the privilege of the sacrifice, and I cannot bear to see it happen. "But first we must go to the foreigners' camp and say good-bye to Ly-iss."

"Ly-iss!" Quangatarask sings. "When, now?"

"Just after sunrise tomorrow," I promise him.

The morning is frosty, but by midday we can kick off our moccasins and Father Sun will warm our backs, for we are nearly at the season of the budding of leaves. Quangatarask walks the whole way himself. What a welcome change that is!

At the Jamestown fort Ly-iss seems to be waiting for us. I am shy about talking to him since the day of the burning of our village. My feelings are very confused; his, too, I suppose. Quangatarask knows nothing of that, and so he runs right to Ly-iss, whose good nature seems to have forgiven me for my harsh words that terrible day.

He has changed much in the seasons I have known him. He is not tall and straight like Lightning nor is he squat and rutted like Deer Knife. He is . . . just . . . Ly-iss. To prepare for my time with the Dream-Reader, I have spent many hours, even days, in the temple and steam house, praying and opening my heart to the words of the Spirits. Something has changed. I hear their voices more clearly, and I see more deeply into the souls of people who bare themselves to me. Ly-iss is an open door, inviting entry.

"What do you see in me?" he asks now.

Much that I cannot say. "You will go back to your homeland." I do not tell him about the hardships of his family or the struggle he will have in leaving them behind to return to these shores or the sleepless nights and heartbreak. I pass through all that and simply tell him one truth: "Someday you will come back as a great medicine man."

I also tell him, "In a day's time I will go to the *hobbomak* for my dream vision, and if it goes well and the Spirits are willing, I will go on to Werowocomoco to learn with the Dream-Reader."

"This will help you as a healer?"

"I have seen miracles."

"Then you must teach me what you learn."

"Not so simple." Afterward it will not be suitable for me to wander freely and visit foreigners, but I do not tell him that either. "We will meet again," I say, although I am not sure I can keep the promise. "When I am chief of the Pamunkee!" Yes, as a chief I can welcome anyone, Indian and English alike.

A smile spreads across Ly-iss's face like a slice of sunlight, and I do not know what else to say, so I pull Quangatarask off the stable door and gather my things for the walk back to Menapacute.

"*Anah*, Ly-iss. That means good-bye in my language."

"My people say fare thee well."

My heart hangs heavy in my chest, for saying good-bye to Ly-iss is saying good-bye to my father yet again. I peel Quangatarask away, as always, and we take the first steps on the journey to my future as a Dream-Reader.

We are not yet out of the fort when Ly-iss comes running up to us. "One thing I wanted to tell you, Sacahocan, to set the record straight. Captain Smith? The man you call our *weroance*?"

"Yes, your father," I sigh, remembering him dragging Chief Opechancanough into our village and giving the order that set our homes and crops on fire.

"That's just the point. He's not my father at all."

"Not? Oh! So much better!"

"I agree! So . . . *anah*, Sacahocan."

"Fare thee well, Ly-iss, until we meet again."